A HOME FOR
TEASEL

Look out for more by
Margi McAllister

❦❦❦ **FAWN** ❦❦❦

A HOME FOR
TEASEL

Margi McAllister

SCHOLASTIC

First published in the UK in 2013 by Scholastic Children's Books
An imprint of Scholastic Ltd
Euston House, 24 Eversholt Street
London, NW1 1DB, UK
Registered office: Westfield Road, Southam, Warwickshire, CV47 0RA
SCHOLASTIC and associated logos are trademarks
and/or registered trademarks of Scholastic Inc.

Text copyright © Margaret McAllister, 2013

The right of Margaret McAllister to be identified as
the author of this work has been asserted by her.

ISBN 978 1 407 13106 1

A CIP catalogue record for this book
is available from the British Library.

Printed and bound by CPI Group (UK) Ltd, Croydon, CR0 4TD
Papers used by Scholastic Children's Books are made from
wood grown in sustainable forests.

1 3 5 7 9 10 8 6 4 2

This is a work of fiction. Names, characters, places, incidents and dialogues are
products of the author's imagination or are used fictitiously. Any resemblance to
actual people, living or dead, events or locales is entirely coincidental.

www.scholastic.co.uk/zone

For Emily, with love

This book is also in memory of Planxty Oscar, a very
good-natured horse who belonged to my sister.
In Shakespeare's Richard III the king shouts,
"My kingdom for a horse!" If the horse was
Oscar, he'd have got a very good bargain.

The authors thanks go to:
Helen Dinsdale,
Julia Gibson,
and Tamzin and all the crew at
Hebden Bridge Equestrian Centre.

Here she is

In the fading sun of an afternoon in winter, a pony stands alone in a field. Teasel is light biscuit-gold, and now that the weather is cold her coat is thick and soft. Her pale flaxen mane sweeps softly to one side, and she stands very still with one hoof tilted, resting a hind foot. On the other side of the fence stands her companion, Hattie the donkey, with her waterproof cover over her back.

Deep in the pony's bones are the memories of her past and her ancestors. They tell her of a hillside where clover grew in the grass and the breeze was sweet to breathe. She can taste the springtime. She dreams of spring and summer.

When the back door of the house opens with a click, Teasel flicks her ears forward and tosses her head so that her long mane ripples. Her herd mother, Arabella, has come to see her, to talk to her and feed her the crisp sweet carrots she loves. She fastens the warm rug over Teasel's back, pats her neck, and smooths her. Teasel always loves this time of day, but today it feels wrong somehow. She shudders.

Arabella's out of breath today, and that isn't right. Teasel can feel her heart flicker and hurry. It wasn't like this years ago, when she and Arabella had rescued each other from darkness. For the first time since Arabella brought her home, Teasel is afraid. Nervously she shakes her mane.

Drops of rain fall in the twilight as Arabella goes back into the house. Sadly Teasel puts her head down. Change is coming, she can feel it in Arabella's breathing and her heartbeat, and Teasel does not want change. She waits, and stamps a hoof. What will the next day bring?

Chapter One

Gwen arrived home with her hair wet from the rain and her clothes smelling of damp dog. Mum was picking the twins up from Cubs, Dad was still at work, and Charlotte, two years older than Gwen, was hunched up in front of the computer doing something she said was homework, though Gwen could see that Charlotte was Facebooking her friends as usual. The house was quiet, which was so unusual, it felt weird.

"Where have you been?" asked Charlotte, looking her up and down.

"Walking the labradors by the river," replied Gwen, and brushed white hairs from the school trousers that she wasn't supposed to wear for dog walking.

Charlotte wrinkled up her nose. "You smell like a wet puppy," she said, and turned back to the screen.

Gwen sighed. Charlotte didn't have a clue. She went to her room, changed, and opened the top drawer of her desk.

A few sketches were in there, some of them unfinished. Gwen knew she wasn't all that good at drawing but she loved to do it, especially drawing horses. She could never quite get the angle of a hoof right, or the curve of a horse's back, but she spent hours trying. There were a few old Christmas cards in there and, kept neatly in its plastic case, her building society savings book. She smiled as she slipped her dog-walking money between the pages. Every little helped! Then she moved a heap of old *Your Pony* magazines from her chair, pushed away a half-finished sketch of an Arab mare, and pulled her homework diary out of her school bag.

Today's homework didn't look so bad. It was something about farming and the environment, so it gave her the chance to write about animals. She added a few more details to the sketch, pushed her floppy ginger hair behind her ears, and began to work.

The sound of a piano exercise reached her, so she got up and closed the door. Charlotte played very well, but it put Gwen off her homework. Charlotte was the clever one, the pretty one, and the musical one. If it wasn't the piano it was the violin, and if Charlotte was coming up to an exam she played the same pieces day in, day out, until Gwen could still hear them when Charlotte was asleep. Gwen had never taken to music. Mum and Dad said it was just as well, because music cost a bomb.

As for the twins, Robin and Jack, there wasn't much

chance of either of them being musical. At seven years old they didn't do tuneful, they just did noise – too loud, too often, and too much. Jack was all right, but all the same, their world was to do with sport, loud noises, and food. Oh, and Robin's asthma. If ever Mum and Dad tried to get him to do anything he didn't like, he just started wheezing.

And Gwen? When she had been a small child, Dad had called her his little golden-haired princess. She still had the red-gold hair and the pale skin that went with it, but she was pretty sure that real princesses didn't have freckles, and she had lots of them. She was so used to jokes about "gingers" that she hardly noticed them any longer. She was used to her freckles, too, and didn't worry much about what she looked like.

The main thing in Gwen's life was animals, and especially horses. Why play a piano when you could be running about throwing a stick for a dog, or riding a horse? The only thing she wanted, all she had ever wanted or asked for, was a pony.

A pony, said Mum and Dad, was out of the question, but that didn't stop Gwen from longing and hoping for one, and, now and again, begging them to think again. They had told her over and again why she couldn't have one. They'd argued about it so much that Gwen could repeat it all in her head like a lesson she'd learned by heart.

Ponies are expensive. So are vet's bills, food, farriers, saddles and bridles, and rent for somewhere to keep them. . .

One day, Mum had been angry and said, "Money doesn't grow on trees, you know, and neither do ponies!" and the whole family had laughed about it for a week. But mostly, Mum and Dad just said, "Ponies need exercise." (*But that's the point*, thought Gwen, *I don't want to just keep it in a field and look at it!*), and, "You need to know how to look after a pony." (*But I do know how to look after a pony!*)

They had offered her other animals. They had decided that a dog would be too big, too energetic, and too much trouble, and Charlotte and Robin were allergic to cats, but would she like a rabbit or a guinea pig? Gwen had replied, with tears of frustration in her eyes, that rabbits and guinea pigs are all very well to cuddle, but what she wanted was a pony, and finally Dad had lost his temper.

"None of us can have everything we want!" he had said, and Gwen had stormed off to her room and banged the door so that nobody could see tears in her eyes. There was no "everything" about it! Charlotte had her violin and her piano, and at seven years old, the boys had so much games stuff and Lego that you couldn't open a cupboard without it all falling out. For Gwen, there was only one thing in the world that she wanted.

When she had been very little she had loved stories about princesses, but her favourite princess books were the ones where the princesses went riding, usually on white horses. As far as Gwen was concerned, a princess should have a beautiful pony and ride it every day. As she got older, she became impatient with stories of princesses who sat around waiting to be rescued by a prince. Any decent princess should be able to look after herself by jumping on to her horse and galloping out of danger. If it was a magical horse, maybe a flying horse, all the better. She drew pictures and made up stories about princesses and their magical horses, horses that could fly into the sky with a toss of their manes. Eventually she lost interest in the princesses, but not the horses. And they didn't have to be magic, or even beautiful. Just horses.

One summer, when she was nine years old, horses had stepped out of her dreams and into her life. They'd had a family holiday in a cabin in the Lake District, and she'd gone pony-trekking, usually on a quiet, shaggy old pony called PJ. After every trek she'd hung around at the stables, helping to muck out, brush horses down and hang nets of hay in the stables. She'd learned how to clean a horse's hooves, saddle up, and approach a horse without scaring it. If she was lucky, she got an extra ride. Sometimes that was after the saddles had been taken off and she had learned what a sharp backbone a pony has, but she hadn't minded that. Her family had gone back there on holiday again, and those times had been the high points of her life. She still emailed her friends from those stables.

There was a photo of solid old PJ on the pinboard above her desk. PJ wasn't a magical pony for a princess. She was a little Welsh mare, the kind of steady, docile pony that riders call bombproof. Gwen couldn't look at her picture without thinking of a warm old blanket, but with the help of patient old PJ, she had learned to ride, to fall off, and to get back on again.

Mum and Dad had seen how much riding meant to Gwen. They'd managed to book her a few riding lessons but the nearest yard was a long way away and lessons were expensive, so she hadn't been there for a while now. Besides, she never felt that she quite fitted in. She felt at home with the horses, but not with the other girls. They all had their own ponies and had known each other for years. They knew each other's families, too, went to the same Pony Club events, and talked a lot about their new hacking jackets and riding boots, and none of them went to Gwen's school.

She didn't quite fit in at school, either, although she had plenty of friends. There were four of them who sat together – Gwen, Amy, Neeta and Siri – and generally did things together and looked out for each other, but the others weren't interested in horses.

And what even her friends couldn't see was that ponies weren't just there to ride. A pony was a friend like no other. Nobody understood that – not the girls at school, and certainly not her family. But it was no good whining that other people didn't know how she felt about horses. They didn't, and that was that. Gwen wasn't the whining type.

There weren't any fairy godmothers granting wishes. If she was ever to have her own pony, she'd have to do something about it herself. As her nan used to say, "If you want a thing doing, do it yourself." So Gwen went out after school walking dogs, cleaning, doing shopping for people, and earning all the money she could. She'd buy herself a pony, even if it took years.

"Love will find a way," was another of Nan's sayings. *And if love doesn't find a way, I will,* Gwen thought.

She bent her head over her homework again to make the most of the peace and quiet before the boys got home. But they were back before long, and Jack ran into her room to show her his new badge (which was quite sweet of him, really) and sing her his new song (loudly). Then the twins talked non-stop through teatime until Mum said "Ooh!" so suddenly that even Robin stopped.

"I forgot!" she said. "Gwen, I forgot to tell you. When I picked up the boys, Mrs Thingy the Cubs lady asked if you were taking on any more odd jobs, but I said I didn't know. I told her you already had a lot on."

"I can do more," said Gwen quickly. "What does she want?"

"It's not for herself, it's for a woman who lives in the row of cottages on the Littleton Road," said Mum. "She's old and a bit frail, and she needs somebody to do her shopping. . ."

"No problem," said Gwen.

"Don't interrupt," went on Mum. "And odds and ends of things, washing up, hoovering, whatever wants doing."

"I can do that," said Gwen. She wondered if ironing and cooking would be on the list too because she hadn't done those before, but she was willing to have a go. Anything to put more money in the pony fund.

"When does she want me to start?" she asked.

"You can phone Mrs Thingy the Cub lady tomorrow," said Mum, scraping scraps on to a plate. "She'll arrange it for you. It's number seven, the last in the row, Lady Anne Cottages, and the old lady's called Mrs Tilney."

Chapter Two

Lady Anne Cottages on Littleton Road were so far out on the edge of the town that Gwen thought of them as "in the country". Behind them stretched fields and a view of gently sloping farmland, and sheep were distant white bobbles on the moor. There were small pebbly gardens, and a narrow lane leading to a bridlepath ran alongside the end house.

The paint at number seven was peeling, and the windows could do with a clean. Gwen left her bike behind a large spiky bush in the garden and looked for the doorbell, but there wasn't one, and the cat-shaped door knocker was stiff, and squeaked. She was beginning to wonder if Mrs Tilney was in at all when the door began to move jerkily. It seemed as if the person on the other side must be tugging and struggling with it; then, from behind the door, came a voice that completely astonished Gwen. It was a voice that made her think of headmistresses in old-fashioned boarding schools in books, or country ladies with lots of dogs. The sort of voice Gwen and her friends would usually giggle at. A "jolly good show" voice. *Posh.*

"Hang on a mo!" called the voice. "The door keeps catching on this silly old mat. There we are!"

The door rasped open, and Gwen's eyes widened. How could anyone sound so posh and look so poor?

A thin, bright-eyed little woman looked down at her from a face so wrinkled it might have been crumpled up. Her hair was short, straight, and white, and her eyes vividly blue behind glasses held together with sticky tape. Her bony left hand rested on a stick, and trembled a little. She wore a hand-knitted sweater that hung loosely on her – there was a strand of wool unravelling itself at the right cuff – and a tartan skirt with a few stains that might have been tea. A ladder ran all the way down her thick tights to a faded old slipper. From the doorstep she looked down with great concentration, as if Gwen were some particularly interesting insect under a magnifying glass, and smiled. Gwen liked her already.

"You must be Gwyneth, are you?" she asked brightly.

"Gwen," she corrected her. "Mrs Tilney?"

"Oh, silly me!" said Mrs Tilney. She picked up a slip of paper from a table in the dark hall, and held it up to the light. "Gwen Parish. Come in out of the cold, Gwen. Jolly rotten weather, isn't it?"

The hall was cold and unlit, but Mrs Tilney showed her into a room where a small gas fire glowed from the fireplace. Of the four seats in the room – two worn armchairs and two scratched dining chairs – two were covered with heaps of magazines and newspapers, one with books, and a pile of knitting lay on the other one. Gwen didn't like to move anything.

"Just sling the old mags on the floor, dear," said Mrs Tilney. Now that they were on the same level, Gwen saw that Mrs Tilney was just about her own height, which wasn't very big. Gwen was small for her age and sometimes people thought she was younger than twelve, which could get annoying.

"Sit yourself down while I find the shopping list." Mrs Tilney hobbled away at quite a speed for someone so frail. She was back within a minute with a list written in shaky sloping handwriting on the back of an envelope. Gwen read it as Mrs Tilney pointed out items with a knobbly finger.

"Their own brand of biscuits will do, just the small packet," she said. "And Masons's pineapple, it's the only kind I like. If they haven't got Mason's, I don't want any. The smallest tin. Two torch batteries, you know, those little ones. A cabbage and a cauli, both the smallest you can find – and the carrots have to be organic."

"So do you want all the veg to be organic?" asked Gwen, looking at the list.

"Oh no!" She sounded most surprised. "Just the carrots. I used to like popping in and out of shops, but I get out of breath since the winter started." She picked up a battered brown handbag and handed Gwen a ten-pound note. "That should do."

Organic carrots, posh tinned pineapple, cheapie biscuits. . . Cycling uphill was harder now the basket was full. The light was fading as Gwen carried the shopping indoors.

"You're quite sure these are organic?" fussed Mrs Tilney, turning the bag of carrots in her blue-veined hands. "Because the ones with pesticides are no good at all, I can't have those."

"Yes, it says they're organic on the wrapper," said Gwen patiently. She pressed a hand against her stomach, which was growling to remind her that it was teatime, as if she needed reminding. Mrs Tilney sorted through her change and handed back two pounds to Gwen.

"Thank you so much," she said. "Thank you for helping. You're a kind girl. Off you go home, now."

It was a bit embarrassing being called a kind girl. She didn't feel particularly kind, just hungry. Mrs Tilney led the way to the door, stopping to pick up a large black torch from the table in the hall.

"I just need to pop the new batteries in," she began, then, "Oh, bother it!" as it fell apart in her hands. Batteries clanged on to the wooden floor, and Gwen knelt to pick them up.

"Wretched thing!" exclaimed Mrs Tilney.

"Here, shall I do it?" offered Gwen, narrowing her eyes to check that she was putting the batteries in the right way. She couldn't see why Mrs Tilney should need to change the batteries in her torch just at this moment, but she couldn't leave her to struggle in the badly lit hall and maybe drop the whole lot again. "There, that's done."

"Oh, thank you so much, well done!" exclaimed Mrs Tilney. "I can pop down the paddock now and get my little girl all settled down and put to bed for the night."

Gwen felt her heart sink to the pit of her empty stomach. Paddock? *Little girl? Nobody told me Mrs Tilney was a crazy lady. I'm tired, I'm hungry, I've got homework to do, and she wants to wander about outside with a torch, looking for the fairies or something. I can't leave her.*

"Shall I come with you?" she suggested.

Mrs Tilney looked at her for a second or two, saying nothing. She seemed to be weighing Gwen up, making a decision about her.

"Yes," she said at last. "Yes, come with me. I think you'd like that."

I doubt it, thought Gwen wearily, but she managed a smile. She followed Mrs Tilney through the kitchen and a dark utility room, and out of the back door into the chilly evening and the smell of damp grass.

"Mind the step," ordered Mrs Tilney. "Hold the torch. I'll be back in a sec."

Gwen shone the torch. She caught her breath.

In the beam of torchlight stood a golden pony. With her pale gold coat and a fringe of mane above her dark eyes, she shone in the halo of light like a little horse in one of Gwen's long-ago fairy stories. She was too wonderful to be true. She must be part of a dream, and Gwen, watching the large eyes in the elegant face, thought she had never seen anything so lovely.

Mrs Tilney emerged with a wrinkled old apple and the pony turned and walked to her, ignoring Gwen. Gwen knew enough about horses to stand well back from the powerful hind legs of a pony, especially if that pony was nervous because of someone new being there. Instead, Gwen stood beside Mrs Tilney, who was smiling as she stroked the pony's nose.

"This is Teasel," said Mrs Tilney, and it seemed to Gwen that she glowed with love as she smoothed the warm coat. "Do you like horses, Gwen?"

"I love them," said Gwen.

Teasel has not expected this new person. She backs away, swishing her tail. But now the apple is not in Arabella's hand, it is in the girl's hand.

She wants the apple. But she has her pride. She waits to see what Arabella thinks. Arabella is talking to the new girl, calmly and happily, and seems to like her. Perhaps she should try.

Shyly, not sure whether to trust this person, Teasel tickles the apple with her lips. The hand remains steady. The girl stands absolutely still, not jerking or trying to touch her, and Arabella seems pleased, which is a good sign. The apple is good. Teasel crunches it, drops some, and bends her head to pick it up, while all the time the girl stands quietly, letting her take her time.

Curiously, Teasel reaches up and nibbles at this girl's long hair. The girl moves the hair gently away but she does not snatch, or make a noise. She is a calm, gentle person. Teasel waits to see what she will do next.

Gwen watched Teasel's ears. They were pricked forward, so the pony wasn't afraid or upset. She might not mind being approached, now that Gwen had fed her. Gwen stepped forward slowly, gently. She reached out her hand, and touched the warm, soft coat.

"Aren't you beautiful!" whispered Gwen. "Look at you! I didn't know about you!"

"Isn't she a little smasher!" said Mrs Tilney. "She's a bit wary, but she's not laying her ears back, so I think she'll be all right with you. I'll just slip her head collar off."

Mrs Tilney lifted the collar over Teasel's ears and nose and patted her neck.

"Turn your back on her, Gwen, and walk away," she suggested. "See if she's interested enough to follow you."

Gwen did as she said and walked towards the house, biting her lip with hope and excitement. Behind her, she heard the steady tramp of hooves. There was a huffle of warm breath on her neck.

She turned, and stood absolutely still. It was as if she stood on holy ground. Teasel was facing her; the soft brown eyes were watching her from under the pale fringe. Her ears were pricked forward. Hardly breathing, afraid of breaking the spell, Gwen lifted a hand and stroked the deep winter coat. Teasel raised her head.

Gwen remembered something she had read in a pony book. Bending forward, she breathed a long, slow sigh into Teasel's nostrils. Softly, the pony brushed her nose against Gwen's face and shoulder.

Gwen would stroke Teasel's neck again, many times. But nothing again would ever match this first enchanted meeting, when Teasel turned her head and brushed softly against her face, and they breathed each other's breath and agreed to be friends.

"Well done!" called Mrs Tilney. "She's taken a liking to you! Teasel and I rescued each other, didn't we, old girl? She needs her rug on to keep her warm. Could you give me a hand with that? I can do it on my own, but I'm afraid I find it heavy these days. We might get her into her shelter, but if she won't go, she won't. She's an outdoor girl with a will of her own, aren't you, Teasel? Gwen's brought carrots for you! Want to give her a carrot, Gwen? And one for old Hattie the donkey?"

As soon as she got home, Gwen tried to tell the family all about the shabby, refined old lady and the pony. Mum and Dad had been pleased, but between Dad looking things up on the computer and Mum sorting out the boys' games kit for school, they hadn't sat down and listened properly. Jack and Robin had asked her whether she'd been for a gallop, and lost interest when she said that she hadn't ridden Teasel at all. All the same, they got very excited playing at jousting up and down the hall and pretending to fall off, and making a lot of noise. Charlotte had listened for a few minutes, then retreated to her bedroom where she wouldn't hear anything but the playlist on her MP3 player.

They weren't interested. And Teasel was too precious for people who half listened or didn't listen at all, or who thought a horse was only interesting if it was going at a racing gallop with you on top of it. But did that matter? Gwen decided not. It was none of their business. The world of Mrs Tilney and Teasel seemed to be magical because Teasel was in it – and because her family weren't.

By the time her next visit came, Gwen was counting the hours, then the minutes, until she could see Teasel again. When Mrs Tilney gave her the shopping list she dashed round the shop and pedalled furiously back up the hill, desperate to finish all the everyday jobs and get outside to the paddock. But Teasel didn't make it easy for her. She was still not used to Gwen and she showed it, walking away and pretending not to notice her. Gwen stood, pushing her hands into her pockets against the cold, and waited, but Teasel kept her distance. If Gwen took a step towards her, Teasel walked away as if she were deliberately teasing. Gwen could almost see her smile to herself. She laughed softly.

"Is that how it is?" she said. "I can be like that, too. I've got a big sister and two little brothers, and I know perfectly well when somebody's trying to wind me up."

There were still plenty of carrots. Gwen took a pocketful and walked purposefully to Hattie, who stood quietly at the fence.

"Here you are, sweetie," she said. "Want a carrot? Good girl." She let Hattie munch a carrot from her hand, all the time hearing the fast trot of hooves behind her. When Teasel pushed against her shoulder, she laughed again.

"Oh, you want to join in, do you?" She turned and took a carrot from her pocket for Teasel. "I thought you weren't my friend today. Eat that. And here's another one for Hattie. No, don't try and take hers. Don't you dare bully her! Do you want another one?"

She realized it was a long time since she had felt this happy, standing in a field with a donkey and a pony nuzzling at her for carrots. She rubbed her face against Teasel's warm neck, breathing in the familiar smell of horse, and Teasel stayed beside her and didn't seem to mind.

"I'll come here every single time I can, beautiful girl," she said. "And one of these days, you'll be my friend even when I don't bring you carrots."

After that Gwen went to Mrs Tilney twice a week, and at school she would count the hours until she could be there. She always did the boring things first – shop, vacuum, clean the bath – and left the best till last. The best was looking after Teasel, taking her an apple and her rug.

*

She is here again, thought Teasel. *She brings food and warmth, and company too. She talks to me like a friend. She knows my language, she understands how to talk to me. Is she one of my herd?*

She is here again. And again, with my rug. She is putting clean straw in my shelter.

Instinct told Teasel that Arabella was old and becoming slow, and Gwen was young and strong, and it was reassuring to have such a person around. She looked forward to Gwen's coming, and would whinny and trot across the field to meet her.

"You're a godsend," said Mrs Tilney one day when Gwen had cleaned out the dirty straw from Teasel's shelter. "I never imagined finding such a good friend for my little girl. Do you know about how to groom her?"

"Yes, I did that on holiday," said Gwen. "They taught me about cleaning hooves, different brushes, checking for injuries, all of that."

"My dear!" exclaimed Mrs Tilney. "You mean you know how to use a hoof pick?"

"Oh, yes!" said Gwen eagerly. "Would you like me to do Teasel's feet?"

"My dear, I would be so grateful!" exclaimed Mrs Tilney. "My back's shockingly stiff these days, which is such a bore. I've been around horses all my life and I'm not afraid of hard work, my dear, but these days I can just about bend down. And getting up again is another business entirely. Let me go with you the first time, just so Teasel knows she's in safe hands. I know she likes you, but she might be fussy about you looking after her feet. She may feel that you haven't earned the right to do that yet."

A door from the kitchen led to the utility room. As far as Gwen knew, most people used their utility room for laundry, bikes, and gardening things. In Mrs Tilney's, head collars, lead ropes, and a saddle and bridle hung on the walls. At one end, a long kitchen table was covered with battered old wooden boxes.

"Body brushes in this one," explained Mrs Tilney, putting a knobbly finger on each box in turn. "Curry combs here, hoof picks here, saddle soap here." She selected a hoof pick with a green plastic handle and a curved metal hook at the end. "Try that one. Just tell her, 'Teasel, foot up'."

Outside in the paddock, with a carrot in her pocket, Teasel's lead rope looped over the fence and Mrs Tilney standing by, Gwen ran her hand down Teasel's warm, strong foreleg. She had learned to do this at the stables on holiday. *No swellings, no grazes. Good.* She wasn't sure what to do about swellings and grazes, but she knew she had to check for them.

"Teasel, foot up," she said. Teasel did nothing.

"Teasel," she repeated. Teasel still refused to move and Gwen, aware of Mrs Tilney watching, felt her face turn hot with embarrassment. Mrs Tilney came to her side.

"Do what you're told, Teasel, you grumpy little madam," she said. "Teasel, foot up." At once, Teasel lifted her hoof. "That's better. Here, Gwen, take hold of this hoof."

One by one Gwen cleaned the soil from each hoof. By the time they reached her offside hind leg Teasel forgot to be fussy, and lifted her hoof obediently at Gwen's command. Gwen straightened up at last, and patted Teasel's neck.

"She's making you work hard," observed Mrs Tilney. "She doesn't want you to take her for granted, so she's being difficult. Don't worry, you're doing jolly well." Teasel pushed at Gwen's pocket, and, when Gwen offered a carrot, tickled her hand with soft horse lips and made her laugh.

When she reached home, Gwen told her parents all about cleaning Teasel's hooves. They listened politely, but she could tell they weren't really interested.

The next time Gwen cleaned Teasel's hooves it didn't go so well. Maybe she was too confident, and walked round the pony more quickly than Teasel liked. As she ran her hand down a hind leg Teasel gave a swift kick that caught Gwen off balance and sent her sprawling on her back. She wasn't hurt, so she picked herself up slowly and pulled a face. Whatever she had landed in, it squelched. She turned to look. *Oh, dear.* What a pity she hadn't cleaned up the pony poo first. Mum wouldn't be pleased.

"The sooner you get over this pony craze, the better," snapped Mum when Gwen got home and told her what she'd fallen in. After that, Gwen always took a change of old clothes to Lady Anne Cottages – but Teasel never kicked her again.

*

As the days grew longer, there was more time to spend out in the paddock with Teasel. Teasel would trot to meet her, prod her pocket to see if there was a treat in there, and stand still to have the head collar slipped over her ears. There was no lunge rein, so Gwen would clip on the lead rope and walk or trot Teasel round the paddock, wellies squelching in the mud as she ran alongside her. In the rain, when Teasel huddled in the shelter, Gwen would put on waterproofs and splash across the paddock to bring her hay and water. On fine days, while Gwen mucked out and poo-picked, Teasel would canter across the paddock for the joy of it, her mane flying out in the breeze. At the end of each day Gwen would fit the warm rug over Teasel's back, offer her a carrot or an apple, and giggle at the way Teasel nibbled her fingers. She would take carrots and apples to Hattie the donkey, too, but only when Teasel was tethered loosely to the fence or Mrs Tilney was holding firmly to her lead rope. Teasel could be jealous and try to chase Hattie away.

"There's no need for that!" Gwen would tell her. "Hattie's a gentle little soul, leave her alone. She's your friend."

Settling Teasel down for the night, Gwen would brush mud from the golden coat, hang up a hay net in the wooden shelter, and fill the water bucket from the tap in the utility room. Leading her to the shelter she would feel the pony's breath on her face and her mane under her hand, and all the time Teasel's gentle brown eyes watched her from under her mane.

"My word, you're not afraid of hard work!" remarked

Mrs Tilney one Saturday morning, watching Gwen shovel up horse poo and pile it on to the manure heap in a corner of the paddock. "There's an awfully nice chap takes that away for gardens. Jolly good for the roses, isn't it, Teasel? I'll move her to the fresh grass in a few weeks. Scrub up, dear, and I'll make some hot chocolate."

Over hot drinks, Mrs Tilney asked Gwen about the other horses she had ridden and Gwen told her about the pony riding holidays, and steady old PJ at the stables. At first she was afraid of talking too long and too much, but Mrs Tilney was truly interested, sitting forward in her chair with bright eyes and nodding with interest. Now and again she interrupted to say things like "sometimes it's just a case of the wrong saddle", or "bombproof little cobs are good for beginners. Good bone, nice action. I had a super little cob when I was a little girl. . .", and soon they were exchanging stories about ponies that spooked at gates, ponies that bit, and ponies that tried to eat their owner's hair, though Mrs Tilney had far more stories than Gwen did, and more exciting ones, too. Finally, Gwen looked at the clock and Mrs Tilney noticed, and did the same.

"Do you have to go home, dear?" she asked. "I don't want to make you late."

"I suppose I should go," she said, and stood up. "I should have been home half an hour ago, but they probably haven't noticed. I'd much rather be here. My family are . . . sort of . . . well, they're not pony people, I suppose."

"All the same, you must go," said Mrs Tilney, getting

up stiffly. "Tell your mother that it's my fault you're late. I so enjoy having somebody about who likes horse talk."

Gwen smiled. "Me too," she said.

Teasel's paddock was divided into two. Mrs Tilney explained that no self-respecting horse would eat grass that tasted of her own poo, so Teasel was regularly moved from one side of the paddock to the other. As long as she had Hattie the donkey for company on the other side of the fence, she didn't seem to mind. Hattie didn't belong to Mrs Tilney – her owner only rented the field – but, as Mrs Tilney said, they kept each other quiet. They would stand side by side at the fence like children holding hands.

On her next visit, Gwen slipped the head collar over Teasel's soft nose and ears and led her to the other end of the paddock. Hattie trotted along her side of the fence, keeping up with them.

"It's all right, Hattie," said Gwen gently. "Nobody's going to separate you. Now, Teasel, stand still. You could do with a good grooming."

She slipped an arm under Teasel's neck, pressed her face against the pony's soft coat for warmth, and wriggled her fingers into the long, deep mane. Then she began to brush gently and steadily, first with the curry comb, then with the body brush, and all the time loose hairs floated around her and drifted in a golden mist to the grass. Lifting Teasel's long tail aside to brush out mud and tangles, she saw the covering of horse hairs around them.

"You're moulting your winter coat, darling girl," she told Teasel. "Do you know what that means? Spring's coming. That's a good thing."

Teasel knew about spring. She could taste it in the grass and in the air. What Gwen was doing was right, helping her shed the thick layers of winter. And she knew, too, that spring was not just for this even, well-trodden paddock. Spring meant the world beyond the gate. At least, she hoped it did.

There was no longer a time before Gwen. Gwen was part of her world now, as much as Arabella was, but it was Gwen who brushed and soothed her so that she felt smooth and rested. This was her herd, Arabella, Gwen and Hattie. If Gwen wanted her to lift a hoof or stand still, that was a good thing, because Gwen's commands never brought her any harm.

Gwen would never put her in the dark and leave her there, as somebody else once did. If Gwen wanted her to be still it was to give her a warm blanket, or to slip her head collar on or off. She was about food, too – apple and carrot, a fresh net of hay and clean water. Gwen was company, and the sound of her voice warmed Teasel's spirit. The air felt warmer and sweeter than it had for a long, long time, and it was as if Gwen had brought it.

"And I'm going up tomorrow and Thursday to see if Mrs Tilney needs anything, and put the bins out for her," said Gwen. "I'll check the pony while I'm there."

It was Sunday evening, and Gwen was sketching.

She was no longer just drawing "a pony" – now she drew Teasel. The twins were finally in bed; Dad, who was a train driver, was off duty; and Mum was trying to make sense of the following week. She had noted down Dad's shifts, then worked out a way of getting Jack to football and Robin to karate at the same time. Charlotte had a choir rehearsal, a couple of evenings of waitressing, and a piano lesson, and nobody had asked what Gwen was doing this week, so she'd just told them.

"What do you mean by 'check the pony'?" asked Mum.

"Just put her rug on, like I always do," said Gwen. "And hang up a hay net for her, change the water, check her feet, brush her down if she needs it, and poo pick."

"*Poo pick?*" repeated Charlotte in horror.

"Shovelling poo off the grass," said Gwen, and enjoyed the look of disgust on Charlotte's face. "And mucking out the shelter. Everybody who helps with horses has to muck out and poo pick, you use. . ."

"Enough! Please!" insisted Charlotte. "I don't want the details! Do you get paid for all that?"

"No!" said Gwen, but she'd never really thought about it. "I get paid for the housework and shopping, not for anything to do with Teasel."

Mum put down the pen she'd been fidgeting with. "Have you discussed all that with Mrs T?" she asked. "Are you both clear about what's paid work and what isn't?"

"You're always up at her house," remarked Charlotte. "She must be paying you a packet."

"Charlotte, it's none of your business," said Gwen, but she felt uneasy.

"What does it matter?" Charlotte answered back. "I saw her last week in the street, she was giving some poor guy earache for parking in the way of the post office. She had her stick and her wellies, and she was wearing this old raincoat with the hem hanging down." Gwen tried to interrupt, but Charlotte didn't give her a chance. "She looked like a bag lady, but have you heard her, Mum? She's all 'jolly good' and 'I say!' She makes the Queen sound like an Essex girl! And she's got all that land, and a pony! She looks poor, but she must be loaded."

Gwen wasn't going to fall into the trap of losing her temper. She just glared at Charlotte, who ignored her.

"That doesn't follow at all," said Mum. "She might have had a private education, she might have had money at some time, but that doesn't make her rich now. She might have nothing but her pension now. I hope she isn't struggling to make ends meet. She might be too proud to let anyone know. Gwen, you've been to the house, what do you think?"

Gwen thought of Mrs Tilney with her baggy old cardigans and the shabby furniture around her. Come to think of it, apart from the sitting room the house was never very warm – Gwen always left her coat on while she unpacked the shopping.

"She never has anything new," she said, "but I suppose she likes things the way they are."

"Maybe she's just a bit eccentric," said Mum thoughtfully.

"Maybe she's just batty," said Charlotte.

"No, she's not!" cried Gwen, but Charlotte took no notice.

"She's ancient," said Charlotte. "Maybe she's a couple of batteries short of a hearing aid. For heaven's sake, most old ladies have roses in the garden. Or gnomes. She's got Champion the Wonder Horse."

"Charlotte!" said Mum, but there was laughter in her voice.

Typical, thought Gwen. This was always happening. Charlotte would step into a conversation and make the whole thing so funny that nobody could take it seriously any longer, and this time Gwen resented it. It sounded funny, even to her, but that didn't stop her wanting to slap Charlotte.

"She never spends any money on herself!" she insisted. "But she buys organic carrots for. . ." She stopped when she realized what Charlotte would make of this, but it was too late.

"For the horse! Organic carrots for the horse!" Charlotte folded over with laughter. "Does it. . ." she gasped to get her breath back, ". . .does it read the label?"

Gwen looked to Mum for help, but Mum was taking off her glasses and wiping the tears from her eyes. They were still laughing as Gwen banged the door after her and ran upstairs.

It wasn't just the laughter that made her kneel on her bed and give the pillow a thump. It was knowing that, in all that mockery, there could be something true. In spite of her pony and her way of speaking,

Mrs Tilney might be poor, and Gwen hadn't thought of that. Looking after Teasel wasn't like shopping and cleaning, and she'd never wanted to be paid for it. She'd need to talk to Mrs Tilney about that.

Chapter Three

Gwen's next trip to Lady Anne Cottages meant first cleaning the kitchen floor, then cycling through the rain to bring home milk, eggs ("free range ones. My dear, the thought of battery farming puts my blood pressure up"), teabags, bread, and" – Mrs Tilney seemed to dither about this – "er, yes. Bananas. Three bananas. And some of those mints in a tube. Ponies shouldn't really have sweets, you know, but she does so love her little mints and she hasn't had any for ages. The odd treat can't do her any harm. Would you like to give her a mint when you get back? She's so fond of you."

Bless, thought Gwen as she brought the shopping home and unpacked it. What does Mrs Tilney give herself for a little treat? One of those teensy tins of pineapple? A banana?

Mrs Tilney was dozing in a chair by the fire. Gwen hurried outside with the mints in her pocket, her feet squelching in the mud of the paddock. Remembering that it was not a good idea to run at an animal, she slowed down, getting a lot wetter than she already was.

Teasel was in her shelter, pressed against the back. Her head drooped, and at first she looked damp and dismal. But at the sound of Gwen's voice, her ears pricked forward and she turned to look through her fringe like a shy child.

If horses could smile, she would, thought Gwen. Teasel whickered and trotted to meet her and push her face against Gwen's coat. The animal smell of warm wet horse rose from her as she nuzzled and nibbled at Gwen's sleeve.

"Don't eat me," said Gwen, stroking Teasel's neck. "You should have a proper stable with a door, you silly girl." There was a stable in the paddock joining Teasel's, and hoof prints in the mud. "Hattie has a stable. It's good enough for her, so why won't you have one? Hey!" Teasel was pushing at her pocket. "Do you know what's in there? Can you smell mint? Well, if you let me get my hand in my pocket, you can have one. And you needn't think you're getting the whole packet at once."

Teasel was persistent, and Gwen had to push her face away to get the mints out of her pocket, then turn away to open them. Teasel prodded her in the back and tried to eat her hair, and it was like a playground game until Gwen, with wet fingers, managed to get the packet open and offer Teasel a mint from her palm.

There was the soft tickle of horse lips on her hand, then a crunch and a dribble.

"Slobbery girl!" she said, and wiped her hand on her coat. "No, no more. I'm going to get your rug. And your water bucket. Stop it. Get your nose out of my pocket! And you need some more hay." She laughed. She couldn't help it, with Teasel nudging her, nibbling her fingers, her hair and her pocket like a teasing little child. "You do make me work hard, don't you? And I love it, you darling girl. I love every cold soggy moment with you."

By the time Teasel had been settled down for the night, Mrs Tilney was awake and pottering about in the kitchen. Two eggs were rattling in a saucepan as Gwen came in.

"My dear, look at you, you're absolutely sopping wet!" exclaimed Mrs Tilney. "Now, the important thing is, are your feet dry?"

Gwen looked down at her feet. She had left her muddy trainers at the door. Her grey socks – her big toe was sticking out through one of them – were soaked and muddy.

"Get yourself in front of the fire and peel those socks off at once," ordered Mrs Tilney. "It's most important to keep one's feet dry. We don't want you catching pneumonia."

Gwen obeyed, and Mrs Tilney hobbled stiffly away. She appeared again presently with something that looked like a small grey badger but turned out to be a pair of thick woolly socks. They looked tickly.

"There's nothing like a good pair of hand-knitted woollen socks to keep out the cold," she announced. "Get those on, the second your feet are dry. I'll go and get Teasel rugged up."

"I've done that," said Gwen. "And she's had hay and water, and a mint."

"You really are jolly good with her!" said Mrs Tilney warmly. "Thanks awfully."

Gwen bent her head and pretended to concentrate hard on putting the socks on while she fought back a giggle. *"Thanks awfully". People talk like that in those old boarding school stories. I bet she used to wear a gymslip and play lacrosse, whatever that is. And I was right about these socks – they do tickle.*

Mrs Tilney took a purse from her worn old handbag and offered Gwen a handful of pound coins. Gwen pressed herself back in her chair, the way she used to when she was six years old and didn't want to go to bed. She sat on her hands.

"I'm not taking it," she said.

"Pardon?" said Mrs Tilney. Her voice was so stern and low, it was as if she'd heard Gwen swear.

"I love coming here and seeing Teasel," said Gwen. "I can't take money for that. It's not right."

She'd expected Mrs Tilney to try and insist, and urge her to take the money, and she was ready to argue. But she hadn't expected Mrs Tilney to close the purse, put it down, and fold her hands. She looked like a headmistress.

"Young lady," she said, "you came here on the

understanding that you would be paid, and paid you will be. I am not used to being told what's right by a person young enough to be my granddaughter. I hope you don't think I'm a poor old woman."

"No!" said Gwen, feeling her face burn. "No, I . . . I just. . ."

"Or a charity case?" continued Mrs Tilney.

"No!" said Gwen. "I never meant. . ."

"Because if that is what you think," Mrs Tilney went on relentlessly, "you and I will have to part company."

"No!" cried Gwen in dismay. "That's not what I meant!" Wasn't it hard enough at home, with Charlotte and the twins making a cat's cradle of everything she said, without Mrs Tilney doing it too? "It's because I love Teasel! I come here, I get to talk to her and brush her and put her rug on. I keep her clean, and she looks forward to seeing me, she puts her nose in my pocket because she knows I might have something for her. I can't be paid for doing that – I didn't mean to offend you, I'm sorry, but please, don't stop me coming here! It's the nearest thing I can have to a pony of my own. . ." And she astonished herself by breaking down in tears.

She hid her face in her hands, hating herself for losing control. Crying was embarrassing, it was silly, it was wrong, and there wasn't a thing she could do about it. She should never have said those words – *a pony of my own*. It reminded her so painfully of how much she wanted one, and how much, how very much, she had come to love Teasel.

Mrs Tilney did not try to hug or comfort her. She

handed her a large (and, Gwen was glad to see, clean) hankie.

"My dear, there's no need for that!" she said. "Mop yourself up!"

Gwen dabbed at her eyes and sniffed. She sat up straight, hoping to save face.

"Sorry about that," she said as firmly as she could.

"Oh, never mind, dear. I daresay a good howl did you good," said Mrs Tilney. "When my husband died I blubbed like a baby, couldn't help it, and I'm not the blubbing type. Better?"

"It's just that I love being with Teasel so much," she said. "Coming here is the best thing in my life. When I'm not here I look forward to it, all the time. I count the days – I don't know what I did before Teasel, I don't know what I'd do without her. She's my friend. I can't be paid for looking after my best friend." She blew her nose, and went on, "Do you know why I wanted to earn some money?"

"I assume all young people like a little extra pocket money," said Mrs Tilney. "It's a very good thing to earn it yourself."

"It's my pony fund," said Gwen. "I've been saving up for a pony. I know it'll take years, but if I want a pony I'll have to pay for it myself. That's why I took all the work I could get. Only now it doesn't matter so much, because I can come here and see Teasel. I don't just mean *see* her. I mean, the grooming and everything."

"What, even poo-picking in the cold?" said Mrs Tilney.

"Even that," said Gwen and managed a laugh.

"Then I'll just have to pay you for the housework and not for looking after her," said Mrs Tilney. "Is that a deal?"

"That's great, thanks," said Gwen and handed back the hankie.

"Good," said Mrs Tilney. "Buck up, then."

As Gwen's eyes cleared, she saw that Mrs Tilney was looking thoughtfully at her feet.

"Socks a good fit, are they?" she asked.

"Yes, they are," said Gwen. "And they're warm." The tickling was wearing off.

"What size feet do you have?" continued Mrs Tilney.

"Three," said Gwen. "Three and a half if it's a narrow fit."

"Jolly good," said Mrs Tilney as if she approved. "Pleased to hear it. There's your money for the housework and shopping, and let's have no more nonsense about it. You'd better take yourself home now. Your mother will think I'm holding you to ransom."

"Can I say goodbye to Teasel?" asked Gwen.

"Of course you can, but put my boots on. They're at. . ."

Something screeched, so loud and shrill that Gwen ducked, even as she realized what it was. Mrs Tilney looked up at the ceiling as if it might fall in.

"What. . ." she began.

"Smoke alarm!" shouted Gwen. She ran to the kitchen, turned off the cooker, and threw open the door to the utility room, then the back door, to let the smoke out. A drift of smoke rose from the saucepan where the eggs had stuck to it.

"Don't touch that pan!" she yelled over the screaming alarm as Mrs Tilney followed her into the kitchen. "Let it cool down! The eggs boiled dry!"

"But how can we stop that racket?" shouted Mrs Tilney. "Can't we turn something off?"

"No, we can't," said Gwen, who was used to this. Everyone at home liked crispy bacon sandwiches, so the alarm went off all the time. "You just have to open the doors and windows to let the smoke out and bring the heat down."

"I don't know," grumbled Mrs Tilney from behind her. "I suppose we have to have these things, but why do they have to be so noisy? Can't they just ping quietly instead? Is there a switch to turn it down, at least?"

Gwen looked away because she couldn't help smiling. "They have to be loud so you can't ignore them," she said.

"Well, you certainly can't ignore *that*," said Mrs Tilney firmly. "They can hear it in Paris! My nephew told me I needed to have one of those beastly things, but he didn't tell me it would sound like a. . ."

The alarm stopped in mid shriek.

". . .a banshee!" yelled Mrs Tilney into the sudden silence. "Thank goodness for that."

With an oven glove, Gwen picked up the pan and ran cold water into it. Volcanic steam sizzled into the air.

"We can shut the door now," she said, because a cold

draught was sweeping through the kitchen. "It's a pity about your eggs."

"Oh, well, I was only boiling 'em to get the things used up," said Mrs Tilney, pulling the door shut. "I much prefer sardines, but I don't like waste." She peered into the clouds of steam. "Will they come off the bottom of the pan, do you think? I suppose something in here will scrape them off." She rattled around in the cutlery drawer. "If all else fails, I daresay we can prise 'em out with a hoof pick."

"A *hoof pick*!" repeated Gwen. "Teasel!"

She ran to the doorstep and called Teasel's name. There was no whinny, no stamping of a hoof, no huffle of breath. No Teasel. The paddock was empty.

"Teasel's gone!" she called. A pair of long black boots stood at the door, so Gwen pushed her feet into them. "I'll find her!"

"Take the torch!" urged Mrs Tilney, and hurried along the hall to fetch it. Gwen grabbed it, ran into the paddock, raging at herself for not thinking of this sooner.

"I'm sorry, I'm so sorry!" gasped Gwen. Shining the torch into the fading light, she saw only hoof prints. "She's jumped the fence."

"I don't know what you're sorry about," said Mrs Tilney calmly. "It's not your fault."

"It is, because I opened the back door," she said. "I should have thought. I knew that horses hate loud noises. I'll find her."

She grabbed a head collar, climbed the fence and

ran into the dark lane, taking one last glance over her shoulder at Mrs Tilney, who stood with her hands tightly clasped and a little furrow of fear on her face. Mrs Tough-As-Old-Boots, Mrs Down-to-Earth, had turned into a little knot of anxiety.

Teasel looked about her for something familiar, but there was nothing, and she was separated from Arabella, Hattie and Gwen, her herd. That was frightening. Something bad had happened. There had been a horrible noise, too high and too loud, and it wouldn't stop, and all she could do was run, clear the fence, and keep on running. Now, everything about her was strange.

It was a long time since she had galloped, and now that she had stopped she was shaken and troubled. There was sweat in her coat. She neighed to call her friends, but nobody answered, and she hated being alone. She wandered one way and another, wondering how to find home. One foreleg was painful.

As the panic wore off, she sheltered near a tree. Someone might come for her. Somebody must. Miserably, she lowered her head.

Gwen stood in the lane, cast torchlight about her, and called for Teasel, but her voice sounded thin and tiny against the late sky and the wide dark land. She listened, hoping for the steady beating of hooves, but there was nothing. Teasel couldn't have jumped the hedge into the next field. When she'd cleared the fence into the narrow lane, she couldn't get enough of a run up to jump anything else, so she must have stayed in the lane. Which way had she gone? There were prints, and with a surge of relief Gwen saw that they led towards the bridlepath and the moor, not the main road. Gwen ran along the bridlepath, stumbling in the unfamiliar boots, running until her chest hurt, following the hoof prints, calling Teasel's name.

She had never been on this path before, but at least it *was* a path, and she kept her eyes on the beam of torchlight. The hoof prints led uphill on uneven ground, and she splashed through puddles. Twice, she turned her ankle. She called out again and stood still to listen, frowning with concentration. Something in a tree rustled, and from far off came the harsh bark of a fox. Then, to her joy and relief, came a soft whinny.

"Teasel!" she cried. "Teasel, I'm coming!"

Teasel lifted her head, and her ears twitched forward eagerly. Gwen! Gwen had come to find her! She took a step or two forward in hope. Gwen would know the way home, and lead her to safety with Arabella and Hattie, her own paddock and her shelter, and all would be well again. She whinnied to tell Gwen where she was and tried to trot toward the sound of her voice – but trotting hurt. Her foreleg was painful when she put her weight on it, so she could only walk, and she did that unevenly. Slowly and as steadily as she could, she walked down the hill to the sound of Gwen's voice. The ground was wet and stony but she plodded on, knowing that soon the terrible loneliness would be over. She would be safe as soon as Gwen's hand was on her shoulder.

Deep inside her, Teasel knew that there was another kind of life, a life lived with other ponies with no Gwen and no Arabella. But not here. This was not a safe place to be alone, with unfamiliar noises around her, and high hedges and fences to keep her from running home as directly as she could. *Gwen, Gwen, come for me. Everything will be safe when you are here. Find me, hear me.*

Scrambling towards the sound of Teasel's whinny, Gwen heard the uneven hoof beats. Then there was a "harrumph" as Teasel blew down her nose and walked into the torch beam, and relief made tears prickle behind Gwen's eyes. Here she was, Teasel, in a halo of light, just as when she had first seen her. She was safe. But she might be lame, and must be terrified.

"Come on, then, sweetheart!" called Gwen. She nearly broke into a run, but remembered just in time not to run at a frightened pony. "Good girl! Darling girl, what's happened to you?"

Teasel stepped forward and stood contentedly at Gwen's shoulder. Gwen patted her neck, smoothed her and hugged her, feeling fear in the quick heartbeat under her hands.

"You're all right," she said softly. "You're safe. Poor Teasel, were you terrified? Sh, now, darling girl. Gwen's here. What's the matter with your leg? Is it your hoof? Let me see. Teasel, foot up."

She ran her hand down Teasel's leg. Teasel flinched and stamped, and Gwen stepped back, shining the torch. A dark stain was already drying against the golden coat.

"Poor Teasel," she said. "Let's get you home and see what we can do with that. Mrs Tilney will know."

She patted Teasel's neck, then wrapped both arms round her and hugged her. Feeling the warm, soft neck against her face, the happiness of finding the pony flooded into her and she pressed her face against Teasel, curling her fingers into the long mane. "Darling girl, stay safe," she said. "I love you too much for anything bad to happen to you."

She could have stayed there for hours, pressing her face against the pony's neck, holding Teasel in her arms. The heartbeat steadied and became strong and rhythmical, filling her with peace.

But they had to get home. She slipped the head collar over Teasel's nose and ears, clipped on the lead rope, and clicked with her tongue to make the reassuring sound Teasel liked.

"Let's get you home," she said. "Mrs Tilney's worrying about you. Teasel, walk on. Good girl."

All the way home, through the mud and the rain, she talked to Teasel, calming and steadying her – "and there are the lights, can you see, Teasel? That's the house. Look, there's Mrs Tilney out waiting for us!" She raised her hand and waved. "She'll know what to do about your leg. Home now."

Mrs Tilney stood in the light from the open doorway.

She raised a hand to wave, then disappeared back into the house. By the time Gwen and Teasel reached the paddock she was there in a long waterproof coat and wellies, opening the gate.

"Well done, dear!" she exclaimed, patting Gwen on the back. She stroked Teasel's neck. "Silly girl, running away like that!"

"She's scraped her leg," said Gwen as she led Teasel through. "I don't know what to do about that. Should I just wash it down?"

"I'll take a look at it with you," said Mrs Tilney. "It's the sort of thing you need to know, if you're going to hang around with horses. Wash your hands before you touch the injury. Let's have the torch."

When Gwen had washed, she crouched down in the damp field to look at the scrape just above Teasel's knee. It wasn't bleeding, and there was no swelling.

"It's nothing to worry about," decided Mrs Tilney. "It just needs a gentle clean, just water and a sterile cloth, as you would if it happened to you. I'm not a great believer in ointments and such like. Keep it clean and dry, and we'll watch in case anything nasty develops – but I doubt it will. She's a tough little outdoor girl, aren't you, Teasel?"

Mrs Tilney held the lead rope and urged Teasel to stand still while Gwen gently patted Teasel's graze clean. She remembered the way they calmed Robin when he was having an asthma attack.

"Shh, shh," she said softly. "That's it. That's it. Well done."

With every second she felt colder, but she couldn't leave Teasel without a good grooming. "I'll brush her down," she said. "But I'd better phone home first in case they're worried."

"No need," Mrs Tilney told her. "I rang them earlier, to let your mum know you'd be late. Told her Teasel had gone charging off and you were rounding her up. There's time for a hot drink before you go home. I should think you could do with one."

Gwen nodded her head. Her fingers were so cold she could hardly handle the hoof pick, but finally Teasel was brushed, rugged and settled for the night. In the sitting room Gwen and Mrs Tilney sank thankfully into saggy chairs by the little gas fire, and sipped hot chocolate. Gwen warmed her hands on the mug, and Mrs Tilney rearranged the damp socks that were steaming by the fire.

"Boots fit all right, do they?" asked Mrs Tilney.

"Oh, sorry!" said Gwen. She had meant to leave them at the back door, but they fitted her so well that she'd forgotten she was wearing them. She stood up. "I'll leave them at the door."

"But do they fit?" persisted Mrs Tilney.

"Like gloves," said Gwen.

"Good," said Mrs Tilney. "Riding boots. No point in spending money on a pair when you can wear mine."

Gwen nearly said that she didn't need riding boots. Then she thought of what Mrs Tilney might mean, and after that she didn't dare say anything in case the wrong words came out.

"Well, somebody has to ride Teasel," said Mrs Tilney. "She doesn't have nearly enough exercise just pottering about in her field, and she must get bored. And I can't see me riding her out again!"

A shiver of hope ran down Gwen's spine. She couldn't quite believe it.

"You want me to ride her?" she whispered.

"No, girl, I want you to give her away to a travelling circus!" Mrs Tilney said impatiently. "Of course I want you to ride her!"

Gwen tried to speak, and couldn't.

"Now what's the matter?" demanded Mrs Tilney.

"I don't. . ." Gwen swallowed hard and tried again. "I don't know what to say. It's like a dream. My big dream."

"Nonsense, girl, it's just riding a pony," said Mrs Tilney brusquely. "And I'll be very glad if you do. So will she."

"Thank you," said Gwen, but it didn't seem like enough.

"Thank *you*," said Mrs Tilney. "If I didn't have someone to ride her, I suppose I'd have to sell her."

For the first time, Mrs Tilney's voice sounded a little frail. Were her eyes filling?

"Oh no, don't sell her!" said Gwen.

"No," said Mrs Tilney softly. She folded both hands tightly over the top of her stick. "I don't think I could bear to part from her now."

Gwen nodded. She could understand that. How terrible to have a pony, and then lose her!

Shyly – because she didn't want to seem nosy – she said, "You told me once that you and Teasel rescued each other."

"We did," said Mrs Tilney. "She was my lifeline, and I suppose I was hers." She gazed thoughtfully at the fire over the top of her mug, wriggled more comfortably into her chair, and said, "It was just the time when I needed her. You see, my dear, there were always ponies when I was a girl. My sister and I each had one. At school most of the girls had ponies, that's just the way it was. Dogs and horses. When I grew up I worked as a nanny in country houses where all the children had dogs and horses. I spent years working at Haspin Hall, Lord Kendal's place, looking after his children and their ponies. The smallest boy had a sweet little Shetland that nearly choked itself by bolting its food down, and I had to call out the vet.

"I was expecting the usual vet, the old one, because he was always the one who came, and Lord Kendal was most offended if they ever sent anybody else. But I suppose the old vet must have been out on some other emergency, because they sent the new young chap instead. My dear, I nearly dropped dead at his feet!"

Gwen smiled. It all sounded like a different world, but she could imagine a young Mrs Tilney with a Shetland pony on a lead rope.

"Well, now, to cut a frightfully long story short, I married him," went on Mrs Tilney. "And we had such a life! Jeremy was a jolly good horse vet and we did a few years in Canada, but he wanted to work with big cats, too, so we went to Africa. Then the old buffer who owns the Greatwater Estate decided to open a safari park, and asked Jeremy to come and work for him. We never had children, but there was always some creature or another to look after. Sometimes there'd be an orphan tiger cub or two in a basket, and of course tiger cubs stalk everything, including each other, so I was forever falling over them, but they were most awfully sweet. They needed looking after, like all babies."

This time Gwen pictured the young Mrs Tilney with a tiger cub in her lap. The tiger cub would know it was in safe hands.

"When Jeremy became ill," continued Mrs Tilney, "I thought, well, we've had forty-seven years and it's been good. We can't complain now. I kept him at home as long as I could. I had nurses coming in, we had stairlifts and hoists and goodness-knows-what. Oh, not in this house," she added, as Gwen looked about her. "That was a much bigger house, and after Jeremy died I felt lost in it. And it was dark. I don't mean really dark, I mean, you know, I *felt* dark. Dark inside. Everything felt dark. Dark grey. Do you know, dear, I just didn't care about anything any more. All those lovely years, all those animals – it was as if I lost all of my past when I lost Jeremy."

Tears shone in Mrs Tilney's eyes, and Gwen remembered what Mrs Tilney had done when she herself had cried. She pulled some tissues from a box and pressed them into Mrs Tilney's hands.

"Thank you, dear," said Mrs Tilney. She dabbed her

eyes, blew her nose loudly, and tucked the tissues into her cardigan pocket. "Then one day, when I was feeling absolutely rotten, my nephew Michael telephoned me. 'Whatever you're doing today, Auntie, stop it,' he said. 'I'm coming to pick you up this afternoon and we're going on a mystery tour.'

"That was most unusual. It's a long drive for Michael to get here, and he's a very busy man. He came with the car that afternoon, and we drove out to a pony rescue centre, of all places! My dear, Jeremy and I used to go riding together right until he was ill, but it was years since I'd owned a pony. Michael doesn't have a clue about horses himself, doesn't know one end from the other, but he knew that I used to ride. He drove me to Pony Rescue and said, 'Now, Auntie. They all need good homes. What do you think?'"

"And what did you think?" smiled Gwen.

"I thought it was a ridiculous idea," replied Mrs Tilney flatly. "I had no idea of taking on another pony at my age. I didn't have anywhere to keep it, for a start. And then I met Teasel, and she just looked at me. You know what I mean."

"Oh, yes," said Gwen. She knew that look, the way Teasel's soft brown eyes look out from under the pale fringe of mane.

"Then they told me her story," she said.

Gwen leaned forward. This was what she most wanted to know.

"She's a Welsh hill pony," said Mrs Tilney. "For the first couple of years, she lived wild on the hills in a herd. When I say 'wild', all those hill ponies have owners, but apart from making sure they don't come to any harm, the ponies are left to look after themselves. When they're old enough to have a bit of sense, they're brought down from the hills to be sold at auction. Teasel had been brought down from the hill, sold, broken in, and sold again. Unfortunately, she ended up with some people who should never have been allowed to keep a pony." She narrowed her eyes and tightened her hands until they looked like claws on the top of her stick.

"Were they cruel to her?" asked Gwen. Mrs Tilney frowned.

"It was more ignorance than anything else," she growled. "They didn't have a clue about how to look after her. I don't know why they bought her in the first place. They didn't have time for her, so most of the time she was kept in a stable. They gave her food and water, but she was kept indoors all year round, sometimes all day."

"Poor Teasel!" exclaimed Gwen.

"Finally, they realized that they were a bunch of idiots and sent her to Pony Rescue. When I got there, I took to her at once. I'm small, like you, and she was just a nice size for me, and you know, she is such a darling, isn't she? Then the lady in charge said, 'I'm afraid we have a problem with that particular pony'. I asked her what it was. Was she a biter? A kicker? 'No,' they said, 'she just won't go into a stable. She's been shut away in the dark before, and she won't have it again.' Well, I could understand that! I knew more than I wanted to about being in the dark!

"So that's our story. That's how Teasel and I rescued each other from darkness. I decided I didn't want a big house any longer, so six years ago I sold up and moved here. Less house, but plenty of land for Teasel. But, you see, I can't ride her any more, not with such a troublesome hip. And if I keep her and don't give her exercise, I'm as bad as those awful people who used to have her. Worse, in fact, because they didn't know what a pony needs, but I do. She needs to be ridden, my dear."

Gwen tried to find the right thing to say, and couldn't, so she nodded.

"And if you don't ride her, I'll just have to sell her, won't I?" said Mrs Tilney, and her eyes danced with laughter. "Just as well my boots fit you. Now, you'd better be off, before your mother and father have the search and rescue helicopter out looking for you."

"We were very worried!" said Mum when Gwen got home.

"Sorry," said Gwen. "But Mrs Tilney did tell you I'd be late."

"She didn't say how late! And since when was it up to Mrs Tilney what time you come in?"

"Sorry, we had an emergency," said Gwen meekly, and hugged her. Nothing could spoil her joy today. Dad, who had been talking on the phone, came to join them.

"Yes, she's here," Dad was saying. "She just got here. Thanks." He turned to Mum. "That was Mrs Tilney checking whether Gwen was home and apologizing for keeping her so long. She sounds like a nice old girl. She was very impressed by how well you coped, Gwen."

"No problem," said Gwen with a shrug. Mum couldn't complain after that.

Chapter Four

Gwen tried on the helmet in front of the mirror and smiled at the assured young horsewoman looking back at her. Now she thought about it, she realized that she should have worn it whenever she was with Teasel, just in case of kicks, but in fact it hadn't been on her head since her last riding lesson. All the same, it was undamaged and so was she, and it still fitted. She had her riding helmet, and Mrs Tilney's boots.

There was a knock at the door, and Jack's bright face appeared.

"I drew your pony," he said, and proudly handed her a picture. Gwen smiled. It looked like a small pantomime pony with a small head, a very large body, and one leg shorter than the others, and it stood on vivid green grass under a perfectly round yellow sun.

"It's very good," she said. She gave him a hug and pinned it to the board over her desk. She was fond of Jack. Jack was the twin who didn't have asthma, just as she was the one who wasn't as clever as Charlotte.

"Can I go to see the pony?" he asked hopefully. Gwen was about to say yes, then thought again.

"You'd have to ask Mum and Dad," she said. She wasn't sure about the rest of the family, but she'd be happy to take Jack to the paddock. Jack would feel the way she did about lovely, magical Teasel. "See what they think."

For the first week, Gwen didn't attempt to ride Teasel. She attended to the grazed leg, led her round the paddock, and talked to her all the time. Teasel's numnah, the fleecy cloth that fitted on her back to stop the saddle from hurting, was in the utility room, and when it had been washed and aired Gwen laid it on the warm golden back.

"Let's just get you used to that again," she said. "Then we'll try the saddle. Walk on." And when she had cleaned the saddle and polished it into shining suppleness, Gwen carried it out to the paddock and laid it, heavy and leather smelling, on top of the numnah.

"Please don't throw it off," she said. "I know you haven't worn it for ages, but give it a chance." But Teasel whinnied with pleasure, and Gwen knew that she would have smiled if she could.

The gleaming helmet and Mrs Tilney's old boots

gave Gwen confidence, and she needed it, because she felt it was a point of honour to get easily into the saddle at the first attempt. With Mrs Tilney holding the bridle, Gwen turned the stirrup, gave a bit of a push and a spring, and landed lightly in the saddle, looking forward between Teasel's ears.

"I say, jolly well done!" exclaimed Mrs Tilney. "You're a natural rider! What a good horsewoman's seat!"

Gwen lowered her head and smiled to herself. *Good horsewoman's seat!* It sounded like "a bum the size of a bus", which was one of Charlotte's expressions. She was so glad Charlotte wasn't there to hear it. She fitted the other foot into the stirrup, pressed her heels down, took the reins lightly and clicked her tongue.

"Teasel, walk on," she said.

Teasel stood absolutely still. Gwen prodded gently with her heels.

"Teasel, walk on," she repeated. Teasel lifted one hoof, changed her mind, and put it down again.

"Come on, Teasel!" coaxed Gwen. "You know me! Walk on for Gwen!"

The pony ducked her head down so quickly that Gwen tipped forward and nearly somersaulted over her neck. Teasel pulled up a mouthful of grass and chewed messily at it, as though none of this was anything to do with her.

"She wants you on her back, not me," smiled Gwen. She remembered the way Teasel had made her work for her affection in those earlier days, pretending not to notice her. "She wasn't expecting me."

Mrs Tilney sighed. She moved to the other end of Teasel, and slapped her firmly on the rump.

"Show her who's boss," she ordered. "Pull her head up. Teasel, you idle madam, get moving."

Teasel stepped lazily forward and put her head down, but Gwen, with a firm hand on the rein, raised it again. She gave a little squeeze with her legs.

"Teasel, walk on."

And Teasel walked, slowly at first, as if she were still remembering how to carry a rider. There was a sneeze and a toss of the head and she walked steadily as Gwen, the smile spreading across her face, guided her round the paddock. With a squeeze and a command of "Teasel, trot on", Gwen was rising and falling in the saddle, Teasel's rhythm was her rhythm, and they moved together like dancing partners. She was riding, at last. She was riding beautiful Teasel, and nothing in the world could be more wonderful. With a smile of joy she turned to Mrs Tilney and saw that the lined old face was alight with happiness. Her eyes sparkled. Gwen pulled back a little on the reins, and leaned forward to pat Teasel's neck.

"Good girl," she said. "Well done, girl."

Yes, yes, this was how it should be. The comfortable fit of the saddle on Teasel's back brought back memories of breezes and bridlepaths and the feel of the moorland beneath her hooves. She blew down her nose and sighed, impatient for adventure and life beyond the gate. The bit in her mouth was harder to accept. She did not want anyone putting things she couldn't eat into her mouth. She threw up her head, but Arabella's firm hand somehow slipped the hard metal behind her teeth where it didn't bother her. *And now it's there, it isn't so bad, no worse than having my hooves cleaned or my head collar put on. Nothing to get upset about.* The girth strap became firm and secure around her as Gwen tightened it, stepped back, waited and tightened it again. Teasel twitched her ears. Spring was all around. She could almost hear the buds breaking into green. She snorted and stamped. Life was getting exciting. Hills and new pathways waited for her, and she and Gwen would go together. Arabella was her herd mother, but Gwen was a spark of life and energy in her life. Gwen was the way to new worlds.

Every day that week Gwen rode round the paddock, rising and falling with Teasel's rhythm, guiding her with the reins, urging her to walk, to trot, and to stand, leaning forward to pat her shoulder and neck. Sometimes Hattie would watch, rather like an old man leaning over a fence, but mostly she ignored them. After every ride Gwen groomed Teasel, feeling that Teasel would purr if she could. Patiently, she brushed until Teasel's pale gold coat shone and her mane was like silk. She would settle Teasel at night, talking to her, persuading her to stand quietly and have her hooves inspected. When the first week was over, she rode a little way up the lane, and felt Teasel resisting the tug of the reins when it was time to turn round and come home. *Do I have to go back yet? Already? Can't we go on? I want more.* And as the days lengthened and lightened, they rode out for their first hack on the moor.

In the clear air, on the soft wide moorland, Gwen felt she could reach up from Teasel's back and touch heaven. But wasn't this already heaven? At weekends and in the Easter holidays, only teeming rain and thunder kept them away from the moors. They hacked out on mornings when the world was fresh after rain and Teasel plodded contentedly through puddles. On spring days, after a trot along a bridlepath, Teasel would pretend not to notice Gwen's guiding hand steering her home. Gwen would take her phone, a bottle of water for herself, and a packet of mints for Teasel to nibble from her hand, and when they came to the pure, fast streams she would dismount and watch while Teasel bent her head and drank. High up, far from the houses, the air was so quiet that Gwen could hear the clicking of grasshoppers and the hum of bees on heather.

When Mum and Dad questioned her about the amount of time she was spending with Teasel, and whether she should be doing homework, she gave up all her other jobs, one by one. No more dog walking. No more shopping or cleaning for anyone except Mrs Tilney. She didn't need to save up pony money, not now that she could ride Teasel whenever she wanted to. When Charlotte still complained about the smell of her clothes, she replied that Charlotte should leave her alone, and then she wouldn't notice it. She ignored Robin doing cowboy impressions up and down the hall and making up songs about Teasel, weasel, and measles, and getting Jack to join in. The only thing worrying Gwen was that Mrs Tilney became tired so easily. More and more it was Gwen, not Mrs Tilney, who looked after Teasel – Gwen and Teasel, with the whole summer before them.

On a Saturday afternoon, when a warm breeze stirred the air and petals drifted from the trees, Gwen and Mrs Tilney saddled Teasel up. Mrs Tilney tugged at the girth strap.

"Stay out as long as you like," she said. "She enjoys the exercise, and it's such a lovely day. Remember all the usual stuff, don't get lost, don't go anywhere you don't know. If you fall off, get up and get on again, and leave plenty of time for getting home. Got your phone? Off you go, then."

She put a packet of mints into Gwen's pocket, slapped Teasel on the rump and opened the gate for them. Then she waved her stick heartily in farewell and walked slowly back to the house.

It was the sort of ride to be remembered for ever. When Gwen thought of it afterwards she felt again the well-rounded rightness of it, like a satisfying story, or your favourite meal. On the moors, butterflies settled on the yellow gorse. She heard the rasping of crickets and the brook slipping down its tiny waterfall. Birds sang. Rabbits sat up, looked at them, and dashed away, and a kestrel hung in the sky, sculling the air with its wings. The breeze felt fresh and clean, and everything smelt and tasted of freedom. Freedom washed through her and into her heart and mind. When the sun grew warmer Gwen dismounted and dabbled her toes in the brook while Teasel drank.

"Shall we go on?" she said, when they'd rested. There was a path leading across the moors, and she had often wondered where it led. She mounted, lifted Teasel's head, and clicked her tongue.

No. She didn't hear that word, "no". It was as if she felt it, from somewhere inside herself.

We've already come further than we usually do. Mrs Tilney said not to go where I don't know. And if anything went wrong, I might not be able to get a phone signal up here. . .

It sometimes seemed to her that there was a sensible Gwen and a dangerous one. Sensible Gwen wanted to go back, and it was dangerous Gwen who wanted to ride on, higher and further. But dangerous Gwen was not the right person to be in charge of Teasel. She turned Teasel's head, and the pony obeyed instantly.

That was unusual, and surprised Gwen. Normally Teasel wanted to go on, and pretended not to notice the first tug at her mouth. Today she trotted keenly for home, and Gwen had to hold her back in the slippery and stony places.

"What was all that about?" she asked Teasel as she swung down from the saddle and patted her flank. "Let's get you sorted." She took off the heavy tack, left it in the utility room and went to find Mrs Tilney.

"Mrs Tilney!" she called. "We're back! I've taken her

tack off, but I haven't. . . ."

She had reached the sitting room door, which was open. The high-backed armchair where Mrs Tilney usually sat had its back to the door. Her arm dangled loosely over the side like the arm of a rag doll.

The room felt too still. The house seemed enormous and Gwen could feel the loud, fast pounding of her heart.

She slipped round to the front of the chair, curling her fingers round the phone in her pocket. Mrs Tilney had slumped to one side, her glasses hanging half on, half off, but to Gwen's great relief the eye that was open flickered with a trace of life. One corner of her mouth tried to speak, but the noises made no sense.

Gwen pulled off her jacket and wrapped it round Mrs Tilney.

"You're all right," she said, and repeated it as she tapped three numbers into her phone. *Ambulance first.* She gave her name impatiently and tried to answer questions – "I don't know how old she is, I just do her shopping. Postcode? I don't know, it's just seven, Lady Anne Cottages. The end one. No, other end. Thanks."

Then she made the second call. "Mum, can you come?" she asked urgently. "Mrs Tilney's collapsed!"

She found that her hands were shaking. Outside it had been sunny, but the little house was chilly. She ran upstairs, found Mrs Tilney's bedroom, and dragged a frayed and faded old quilt downstairs to tuck it round the withered figure. Wrapped in the quilt, Mrs Tilney looked like a neglected old doll.

"You'll be all right," she said. "The ambulance is coming. They'll be here very soon." *Oh, I hope so. Please.*

Dribble fell from the corner of Mrs Tilney's mouth on to the arm of the chair. Gwen found a box of tissues and mopped her up cautiously, trying not to get spit on her fingers. She was used to getting horse spit on her hands whenever Teasel ate an apple, but this was different. From the back of Mrs Tilney's throat came a raw, gutteral noise, as if she might be sick. Gwen's stomach churned.

"Don't!" she whispered. "Please, please don't!"

But the noise continued, as if something monstrous had taken over Mrs Tilney's voice. *Pull yourself together,* Gwen told herself. *She's trying to talk.*

"Tell me again," urged Gwen. "It's all right, Mrs Tilney, take your time. Just tell me again."

"I. . . ca. . .," croaked Mrs Tilney. "I. . . ca. . ."

Gwen guessed. "Do you mean, 'I can', 'I can't?' You can't speak? You can't move?"

Mrs Tilney frowned with only one side of her mouth. She tried again, but then, to Gwen's great relief, there was the distant whine of a siren. Mrs Tilney's eyes widened with fear, and with an effort she turned her head.

"Teasel!" said Gwen. "Don't worry, I'll go." If the smoke alarm had terrified Teasel, what would a siren do? She left the back door open and was in the garden, calming Teasel and tethering her to a ring in the shelter when she heard somebody hammering on the door at the front. Mum was there, trailing the twins behind her.

"You two, stay in the hall and don't touch anything," she ordered. "Now, Gwen, where is she?"

Everything was better at once. Mum was good at emergencies. She swept into the room, knelt down in front of Mrs Tilney, and said, slowly and loudly,

"Hello Mrs Tilney, I'm Katie Parish. Gwen's mum. You've been taken ill, but you'll be all right. Can you speak?" She lifted the quilt. "Can you move your hands?"

The siren drew nearer, and Gwen ran outside. She ushered two yellow-jacketed paramedics, a short woman and a tall man, into the house and chased Robin and Jack out of the kitchen.

"It looks like a stroke to me," said Mum quietly, moving out of the way. "Only one side of her face is working."

The paramedics were calm and reassuring, asking Mrs Tilney questions, watching her raise her right hand, trying to make sense of the slurred speech. Jack ran in from the hall to pull on Mum's hand and tell her that Robin had the wheezies again and couldn't breathe, and Gwen knelt by the chair watching the paramedics, angry at herself for being helpless and useless while everybody else seemed to know what they were doing.

"My name's Becky," said the woman paramedic. "Can you tell us your name?"

"U . . . ella," moaned Mrs Tilney.

"It's Arabella," said Gwen. She didn't know how she

knew that, but she knew it was right.

"That's a lovely name!" said Becky. "Now, Arabella, we're going to take you to hospital for some tests. You may have to stay in for a little while."

Mrs Tilney's head jerked so violently that Gwen thought she might be having a fit. Then she realized that Mrs Tilney was only trying to find her, so she took her hand.

"I'm here," she said.

"Eesha!" said Mrs Tilney.

"Teasel?" repeated Gwen, and folded both of her hands round Mrs Tilney's. "I'll take good care of her for as long as it takes. Promise."

"I . . . I ca. . ." slurred Mrs Tilney again. This time, a name slotted into Gwen's head.

"Michael?" she said, and Mrs Tilney nodded earnestly at her.

"That's her nephew," said Gwen. "Do you want us to get Michael?"

Mrs Tilney nodded again. Gwen supposed there must be an address book or something in the house, but she had no idea where to find it, and the paramedics were ready to leave.

"We'll get you into the ambulance, Arabella," said Becky. Desperate to do something useful, Gwen ran upstairs and hunted through cupboards. In a drawer she found a pink cotton nightie, big plain white knickers, a faded dressing gown, and an old framed photograph of a young Mrs Tilney and a tall man with a lion cub in his arms. She picked up soap and a toothbrush from the bathroom and was trying to keep the whole bundle together when Mum appeared at the top of the stairs.

"You want a bag for those," she said quickly. "I'll have to get Robin home – the dust in here's setting his asthma off. The paramedics are keeping an eye on him, but he'll be fine when I get him home."

"I'd better go to the hospital with Mrs Tilney," said Gwen.

Mum seemed to hesitate for a moment, but then she gave a brief nod of her head. "Yes, that'll be best," she said. "She shouldn't be alone. They'll want to ask questions, and you're the one who knows her. When you're finished, give me a call and I'll come and get you. Gwen, where does she keep her keys? No, you can't see the pony today, Jack, we have to get home."

"Thanks, Mum," said Gwen. It wasn't enough – she wanted to thank Mum for coming at a moment's notice, staying calm, knowing what to do. Especially, she wanted to thank her for understanding that Gwen was old enough and sensible enough to stay with Mrs Tilney, not a small child to be whisked away. But Mum would understand that. Gwen saw the disappointment on her favourite brother's face, and knelt down, taking his hands. "I'll bring you to see her next Saturday," she said. "We'll have more time with her then, won't we?" Then she climbed into the ambulance as Becky held an oxygen mask to Mrs Tilney's face.

Chapter Five

"She had a stroke. She could have died," said the doctor.

Gwen sat in a small room in the hospital. They called it the "rellies room" because it was a place for relations to stay when somebody was in hospital. There was a single bed, a washbasin, and a chair. Perched on the edge of the chair, Gwen wiggled her feet and squirmed inside with embarrassment because the doctor was asking her one question after another, and she had to say "I don't know" to nearly all of them. She was about to ask if there was anywhere she could get a drink – it was hot in there, and she was thirsty and hungry – when a nurse opened the door and Mum marched in.

"I went back to the house when Charlotte and your

Dad got home," she announced. "The nephew's called Michael Bailey. I found his number, I called him, and he's coming as soon as he can. Gwen, he said to ask if you'll look after the pony, and I said you had it all organized. Good thing you were there. You did a good job." She pushed a scrap of paper into the doctor's hand. "That's the nephew's number. Anything you want to know, you phone him. Gwen, you can come home now."

Gwen thought longingly of home, and tea, and rest.

"I have to go back first," she said. "Teasel needs hay and water."

"Oh, Gwen," said Mum. "Won't it wait?"

"She's just been exercised, then I left her in the paddock," said Gwen. "I have to go now."

Teasel was confused, and it made her sullen. Gwen had left her alone for a long, sad time after their ride. She had come at last, and looked after her, but where was Arabella? She neighed but nobody answered. So when Gwen finally did come to groom and settle her she was grumpy and unhelpful. She tossed her head crossly, and stamped her hoof when Gwen arrived in the paddock. While Gwen fetched hay and water, Hattie came to the fence to see what was happening, and Teasel chased her away. But by the morning she remembered that she needed company. She whinnied for Hattie and gentle Hattie came to stand beside her at the fence, offering sympathy. Gwen came, too, with apples and mint, and they rode on to the moors, but not far. Gwen was quiet and sad, so Teasel was uneasy, too. Was Gwen the herd mother now? Where was Arabella?

Day after day Gwen arrived, early in the morning and in the evening, to look after her and clean the paddock. Sometimes, they would have a brief ride. Perhaps all would be well, then.

But then new people arrived at the house and came to the paddock to talk to her. She didn't like them.

When Gwen arrived at Mrs Tilney's house on the next Saturday morning, holding Jack by the hand, the front door was open. She tightened her grip on Jack's hand and drew him closer to her, but then clear, cheerful voices came from inside. Gwen relaxed. No need to call the police, then. She didn't know much about burglars, but she was pretty sure they didn't say, "Kettle's on, darling, and I've cleaned the cupboards." A tall, broad-shouldered man with glasses and sandy-grey hair appeared in the doorway with a mobile phone in his hand, and a little blonde woman came to stand beside him.

Something about them looked strange, and it took Gwen a few seconds to work out what it was. Even in jeans and sweaters, they looked smart enough to be in a shop window.

"You must be Gwen!" said the man. He held out a powerful-looking hand. "I'm Michael. Mrs Tilney's my Aunt Arabella. I've heard all about you. Thank you for rescuing my aunt – you did a great job there." The woman smiled and nodded at her. "This is Jill, my wife."

"I'm just making tea," said Jill-my-wife, and beamed down at Jack. "And let's see if we've got any biscuits, shall we?"

Jack glanced uncertainly up at Gwen.

"I think he'd like to see the pony first," she said. "Is that right, Jack? We'll come in presently, when I've had a look at Teasel." From the paddock came the sound of a whinny and she went out to find Teasel, her ears pricked, trotting gladly to meet her.

"Good girl!" she said. "Gwen's here. That's it. Oh, you're my friend today, are you? No sulks? Jack, do you want to come and say hello to her?"

Michael and Jill seemed nice enough people, but she felt uneasy about the way Michael stood at the door and watched her run her hand over Teasel to check for any scratches or swellings. She fetched clean water from the outside tap, but mucking out would have to wait until afterwards. Mrs Tilney never minded her coming into the house straight from shovelling horse muck, but she wasn't sure about Michael and Jill.

"Is she in good shape?" asked Michael. "I went out to her when we got here, but she didn't seem pleased to see me. Neither of us have much of a clue about horses, and I suspect she knew it."

"She's not used to you," said Gwen. "And she's missing her mu— I mean, Mrs Tilney. Jack, stand right back at the door now. I don't want you to get kicked." She picked up Teasel's feet one at a time.

"Is there something the matter with her hooves?" asked Michael. "Does she need new shoes?"

"She doesn't have shoes," said Gwen. It seemed pretty obvious to her. "She doesn't need them. You have to check in case she's got any stones caught or anything. And when the grass is long and the ground gets soft, ponies can get sore feet." She looked down at her hands. Oh dear. She'd need a good wash before she sat down with Mr and Mrs Shop Window.

As they sat and drank tea, they asked her all about how long she had liked horses (*always*) and was she from a big family (*four of us, that's big enough*) and did they all get on together? (*OK.*) It must be very hard work to come twice a day to see to Teasel. (*Not really.*) Didn't she get tired? (*No.* This wasn't quite true, but if she told them she got tired they might tell her to stop coming here.) She found she was sitting on the edge of her chair, curling her hands tightly, glancing nervously at Jack as he dropped biscuit crumbs on the carpet. Michael asked her if she'd been paid.

"I only got paid for the housework and stuff," she said. "Not for looking after Teasel." Then, not wanting them to think that Mrs Tilney was mean, she added, "Mrs Tilney offered to pay me, but I didn't want it."

"Oh." For the first time, it seemed that Michael didn't know what to say. He glanced at Jill for help, but she only shrugged.

"What about the things that Teasel needs?" he asked.

Gwen was glad he'd mentioned that. "We're getting short of hay, and I don't know where Mrs Tilney gets it," she said. "And her hooves need trimming. Mrs Tilney has the numbers beside the phone – for the vet and the farrier."

"We can take care of everything," said Michael with a smile. "Don't worry."

She remembered when she'd last felt like this, nervously perched on the chair and curling her hands. It was a year ago, when she'd been in trouble at school for being late three mornings in a row. It was when Mum had flu, Dad's rotas meant he wasn't at home first thing in the mornings, Robin's asthma was bad and Jack was having nightmares and waking up crying. She and Charlotte had coped somehow, with a lot of arguing. They had always managed to get the boys to school on time, or Robin to the doctor, but every day they were late themselves. The head of year had been very understanding about it, but all the same, Gwen had felt small, like a beetle in a corner. That was how she felt now. Cornered, in the head's office.

"Are you a headmaster?" she asked suddenly, then added, "If you don't mind me asking." But Michael and Jill were laughing.

"Spot on!" said Jill. "And I teach, too, in a college. How did you know?"

Gwen only smiled shyly and shrugged. He was a headmaster, so no wonder she felt like a suspect brought in for questioning. And, what was worse, he was the kind of headmaster who thought he knew the answers to everything. That was going to be a problem. What had he said? *We can take care of everything.* He was good at sorting things out. He would manage everything regarding Mrs Tilney and Teasel. He was listening politely to Gwen, but she knew that he'd already taken over.

"Auntie Arabella will have to be in hospital for a long time yet," said Jill. "And when she comes out she won't be able to look after herself."

Yes, Gwen had already thought about that. Mrs Tilney needed to be in a warm house, without the steep stairs. She glanced down. She'd left her boots at the door, and, oh, rats, she was wearing the socks with the hole in again.

"We really want Auntie to come and live with us," Michael told her. "We both work full time, but we can get carers in."

It was a perfectly sensible idea, Gwen knew that. *It's the right thing for the family to do, to take care of their aunt.* But what would happen to Teasel? Would she go, too? Her face felt hot and she looked down. Now her toes were curling, too, and the stupid white toe poking through her sock was curling over like a baby's finger.

"Unlike Auntie, we don't have a few spare acres of grazing land at the back of the garden," said Michael. (*If you meant that to be funny, it isn't, it's pathetic,* thought Gwen crossly.) "So we can't have Teasel to live at home. But *if* Auntie wants to keep the pony, we can find a livery stable somewhere. You might like. . ."

Gwen jumped to her feet. "Excuse me, please, but I forgot to brush her," she muttered, and dashed out to the paddock to fling her arms round Teasel's neck.

Teasel didn't need brushing, but Gwen needed to

cry. It had been bad enough breaking down when Mrs Tilney was there, but she couldn't cry in front of these smart strangers. She had to get out. She had to hold Teasel and press her face against the silky soft neck, breathing the smell of her deep coat, remembering the first time she had held Teasel like this and shared her calmness. That first time, she had Teasel in the light of the torch as if a circle of magic surrounded her. And she had moved into that magical ring and was held there, with Teasel, for ever.

"It's you and me, Teasel," she said. "I promised your mum."

She could feel somebody watching her. Michael and Jill must have followed her to the door. Couldn't they see that she wanted to be left alone with Teasel? Quickly she dried her eyes on the back of her hand and turned, but it was only Jack who stood at the back door. Watching her, he looked very small.

"Are you crying?" he asked.

"No!" she said, and pretended to laugh. "My eyes got itchy. Do you want to say hello to Teasel? Here, hold my hand."

Jack stretched up shyly. He stroked Teasel with light, gentle fingers.

"She likes you," said Gwen. Teasel didn't even seem to notice him, but she wanted him to feel happy about her. "Do you want a ride?"

He nodded silently and she fetched the tack from the scullery, answering Jack's endless questions as she saddled up. *This goes in her mouth. No, she won't bite* me. No, it won't hurt her. It goes right behind her teeth, can you see? Will you hold that for me? Those are the stirrups – your feet will go in those if you can reach. I'll make them as short as I can. You do it with that strap. You'll need my helmet – it's a bit big, but it'll have to do. I'm not going to let you fall. Finally, with a deep breath and a determined heave, she launched him into the saddle and he grabbed at Teasel's mane.

"Hold on to the front of the saddle," she ordered quickly, and saw the nervous expression on his face as he realized how high up he was. "Don't look down, look straight forward between her ears."

He stared forward with such concentration that she was afraid his eyes would cross. On the saddle, his knuckles were white. He was taking this all very seriously.

"Relax!" she said. "You're safe. Heels down and sit up straight." She clicked her tongue. From above the saddle came a very small voice.

"Don't let her gallop, Gwen!"

"She won't gallop," smiled Gwen, and wondered when Teasel had last had a good flat-out gallop. "Teasel, walk on!"

A slow smile spread across Jack's face as Teasel plodded steadily round the paddock. Gwen smiled, too. This was what it was to have Teasel, to be a big sister to Jack, to introduce him to the experience of riding a horse. Hearing the steady jingle of harness and the soft step of Teasel's unshod hooves, glancing up at Jack's beaming face, she felt that nothing could ever be different. Of course she and Teasel wouldn't be parted. It would be like parting from herself.

She smiled up at Jack. "All right up there? Do you want to get down?"

"Can I go a bit more?" he said.

"Of course you can." Gwen turned her back on the house for another lap. Jack's eyes were shining.

"MERCY ON US, WHAT'S HE DOING UP THERE?"

The yell from Mum made Gwen jump, Jack jerk in the saddle, and Teasel swerve to the left. Gwen caught Jack as he tumbled from the saddle, lifted him away from Teasel's hooves, and sat him on the gate.

"Out of the way, Mum!" called Gwen, because Mum was striding towards them and was likely to be kicked. "Shh! Teasel!"

She brought Teasel's head round, aware of Jack perched nervously on the gate behind her. "Stay there, Jack. Teasel, it's all right. Shh, shh. Good girl. Calm down now. That's it." Teasel tossed her head, but presently she became calm, and stood still.

"What's the matter with her?" demanded Mum. She lifted Jack from the gate and clung on to his hand.

Gwen led Teasel slowly round the paddock to calm her, one hand on the rein, the other gently patting her neck. Mum glared.

"You frightened her, shouting out like that," said Gwen. "Jack's perfectly all right. I wasn't going to let him get hurt. But she couldn't see where you were, and she was scared."

"*She* was scared!" exclaimed Mum. "And Jack might not have been all right, not at all! He fell off! How all right can that be?"

"Can I get on again?" asked Jack eagerly.

"I think that's enough Grand National for one day," pronounced Mum. "That horse doesn't look safe to me, Gwen, not if she does that."

"She's anxious," said Gwen, and didn't bother pointing out that Teasel was a pony, not a horse. "There are people she doesn't know all round her, and she's missing Mrs Tilney. She's stressed, aren't you, Teasel?"

"All right, you don't have to analyse her," snapped Mum. "I just came to pick up Jack and see if Michael and Jill need any help. Are you coming home with us?"

"I haven't ridden Teasel out yet," she said. "I'll be back later."

Jack gazed devotedly at Teasel. He pulled at Mum's hand.

"Can I say goodbye to Teasel?" he asked. Mum glanced warily at Teasel.

"*Please*?" implored Jack.

"Oh, go on then," said Mum. "Gwen, hold on to her . . . head thing, whatever it's called."

Gwen took a mint from her pocket. "She likes these," she said, and crouched down beside Jack. "Put it on your hand for her."

She placed the small white mint on his flat palm and placed her own hand under his. Jack giggled at the touch of Teasel's big, soft lips.

"She tickles," he said.

"That's because she's being gentle," said Gwen. "Next time she sees you, she'll think 'oh, that's the boy who brought me a mint.' Hattie would like one, too. Teasel, leave him alone, you've already had yours. Stay there, Jack, while I fasten her rope to something."

Jack giggled as Hattie crunched the mint, but Gwen could feel Mum's eyes on her back. She wouldn't be happy until Jack was out of the paddock.

"Off you go, now," said Gwen. "Mum's waiting for you. See you later."

When they had gone, Jill appeared in the doorway.

"Are you all right, Gwen?" she asked quietly.

Stupid question, thought Gwen. She didn't like herself for thinking that. Jill was pleasant enough, but it was a stupid question. *My friend Mrs Tilney's in hospital and you're going to take Teasel away, and you want to know if I'm all right?* Her mouth twitched in a way that might have been a smile or might not, and she turned her attention back to lengthening the stirrups.

"You're going to take her away, aren't you?" Gwen said. "I don't mean Mrs Tilney, I mean Teasel."

"Nothing's been decided yet," said Jill. "A lot depends on what sort of recovery Aunt Arabella makes. Clearly, things can't stay the way they were."

Gwen knew she was right about that. It didn't make it any easier.

"I'm taking her out now," she said. "I'll clean all the tack and put it away afterwards."

But as she spoke, she noticed from the corner of her eye that Teasel's tail was lifting. In spite of the way she felt, she wanted to giggle. She knew exactly what it meant, and that there wasn't a thing anybody could do about it. *We're trying to have a serious conversation, and the pony just told me she's ready to go. Well, there's nothing I can do about that.* Into the silence came . . .

Plop. Plop. Plop.

A pause. Gwen waited.

Plop.

It made her think of a clock striking. She folded her lips tightly, but a giggle escaped her.

"I'll clear that up when I get back," she said in the quiet, clipped way that you do when you're trying not to laugh. Pungent steam rose from the fresh droppings.

"No problem," said Jill brightly. "Michael and I can do that." She nodded towards the muck heap. "Does it go on there?"

"Yeah, then somebody takes it away for gardens," said Gwen. "There's a shovel and a stable fork in the utility room. Teasel, stand."

She launched herself into the saddle and gathered the reins with one hand, remembering too late that she hadn't opened the gate. She didn't like to ask Jill to do it, but she'd look silly if she got off, opened the gate, and got on again. But without saying a word Jill walked ahead of her, opened the gate with a smile, and closed it after them. She was a nice enough woman, Gwen decided, but that didn't change anything. These people were planning to take Teasel away.

It was a relief to get out and along the bridlepath. Gwen took one last glance over her shoulder and saw

Michael, in his shop-perfect jeans and sweater, coming out of the house with a garden fork in one hand, marching purposefully towards the horse droppings.

"I hope he slips in it," she told Teasel, stroking her neck. "I hope they both do." She didn't really wish that on them – at least, not on Jill – but she wanted to be grumpy about them. She needed to be angry Gwen, fierce Gwen, fighting Gwen, dangerous Gwen. She talked out loud to Teasel.

"They turn up and think they can take over. I bet they haven't asked Mrs Tilney what she wanted. He just headmastered his way in here. 'Leave it to me, I'm a headmaster, I'll sort it all out, I'll put them all in the right places, and we'll have no more trouble.' Him and his sweetie-weetie wife. I bet she irons his slippers. He'll be giving us all homework next, and asking why we haven't done it." Teasel tossed her head and snorted. "Bless you."

She mustn't allow herself to like Jill much. Jill was part of Team Michael. Headmaster Michael and Jill-my-wife.

"They've got nothing to do with us, Teasel. Well, all right, except that Michael brought Mrs Tilney to you in the first place. But that's just because he was doing that headmaster thing and trying to solve everyone's problems neatly. He'd put us all in boxes if he could."

Boxes? Through the anger, she saw a chance of hope.

"But they can't do that, can they, darling girl? They can't take you away because you don't like being shut in the dark. They'll never get you into a horsebox or a trailer, so you'll have to stay here. There are livery stables not far away, at Dovecote, where you can live in a horse hotel and they'll look after you, and I can still ride you. No, you won't have to go indoors if you don't want to. There is no way they can take you away. Trot on!"

But as Teasel broke into a trot, Gwen imagined her at Dovecote stable and Mrs Tilney far away, living with Michael and Jill. For the first time she felt she was being selfish, wanting Teasel to stay here when Mrs Tilney couldn't.

"You're about nine years old, Teasel, from what Mrs Tilney said. That means you managed for nine years or so without me, so you could be happy without me now. Ponies are always being bought and sold. You belong to Mrs Tilney and she'll want you close. That's if anyone can get you into a trailer."

She tried to concentrate on the ride, the feel of Teasel's steady tread and the way she responded to the gentle guidance of the bit. She didn't want to think of losing her, but at the same time, she couldn't help it.

"You're all I ever wanted in the world," she said as she leaned forward to pat Teasel's neck. It wasn't as if Teasel was just a thing, a possession. She was her friend, and together they shared the wild, airy kingdom of the moors. When they passed the trickling brook, Teasel turned her head hopefully.

"Go on, then," said Gwen. She steered her to the lilting water and let her drink. "Michael and Jill are only trying to help. They want to do something sensible, but it's not just about being sensible, is it? It's about you and me and. . ."

And what? Was it something to do with the ragged, stinging gap that would be left in her life without Teasel?

"Tell you what, though, darling girl," she said. "We don't know what's going to happen, so we'll have the ride of our lives today. You and me, Teasel, when you've just finished drinking all the water in the brook. Take your time, girl."

When Teasel had finished drinking, Gwen raised her head and turned her back to the path. All the moorland lay ahead of them, where grouse and pheasants strutted about and crickets clicked. Teasel trotted forward gladly, tilting her ears, as eager as a little child going to the seaside.

The right-hand path led across the moors on a gentle curve, and with a click of her tongue Gwen turned Teasel towards it. She had got to know the moors in her long rides with Teasel. This path would take them high above the town and bring them home in a wide circle. The taste of the air was fresh and clean, bees buzzed in the growing heather, and where the ground seemed hard, Gwen steered Teasel to the soft turf. The breeze rippled Teasel's mane, and lifted Gwen's hair where it hung below her helmet. The town below them looked so tiny, so like a toy village that Gwen reined Teasel in, and stopped to look at it.

"That's where I live!" she said to Teasel. Far away

she could see her own street, the roof of her house, and the car on the drive. Jack and Robin were helping to carry shopping in, holding the carrier bags up to their chins with both hands. Lady Anne Cottages lay in a row at her feet. She could have been a giant's daughter, reaching down to pick up Mrs Tilney's house and play with it. Somewhere in that toy-box house were Michael and Jill, like the matching dolls in a weather house. But as long as she and Teasel were up here, in their moorland kingdom, nobody had power to hurt them.

"Let's stay up here, Teasel," she said. "Let's stay in our world. I'm the queen of this valley, and you're my magic horse, my flying horse. Trot on."

But there was no need to pretend. It was Teasel and Gwen, the perfect ride, rise and fall, rise and fall to the rhythm and beat of hooves, like a dance. Gwen urged her to a canter. They were together, as if they could read each other's minds, as if they were one creature with the world at their feet and the wide sweep of open moorland before them. Teasel gathered speed, and they flew.

Finally, Gwen pulled gently on the reins. She had ridden out her anger, and knew in her heart that she had been unfair about Michael and Jill. She often thought that Charlotte expected to get what she wanted, just because she wanted it. Perhaps she was doing the same thing herself. She would ride back, and explain politely to Michael and Jill about what would be best for Teasel.

"Good girl," she said. "Yes, I know you want to go on, but I don't want to wear you out. Time to go down?"

Last time they had stopped, she had sensed freedom. Now, everything felt different. The sun had gone behind a cloud, and without the pounding of hooves the silence was strange and unsettling. There was nothing but a snort from Teasel, and her own breathing. The emptiness of the moors felt dangerous. For the first time that day, Gwen was afraid. What if she fell, and was hurt? If she needed help, was there a phone signal here? Would anyone find her?

She remembered the advice in some of the pony books she'd read – *never go riding alone, in case you have a bad fall and can't get help.* Mrs Tilney used to say something like it, too – "Got your phone? Jolly good. If you're not back in an hour and a half I'll send out a search party. We can't have you going base over apex when there's nobody to get you home. Shouldn't really be going out on your own, but I used to do it all the time and I'm still here". Gwen hadn't had a choice – she didn't have anyone to go riding with, and she usually kept to the bridlepaths. She'd never been this far before.

Teasel put her head down to graze, and Gwen let the reins fall loosely through her fingers. If she fell, she supposed she'd get back somehow. Or somebody would find her.

Or would they? How long would it take before anyone realized she was missing? How late back would she have to be?

Sooner or later, they'd notice, she thought, and tried to laugh it off. *At teatime or the twins' bedtime, or when*

Charlotte wants somebody to paint the nails on her right hand. It's the only time she's going to miss me.

It took only a toss of the head and a stamp from Teasel to make her realize that she was feeling sorry for herself. What would Mrs Tilney say if she heard her? Something like, "I say, buck up, girl, pull yourself together!"

The thought made her smile. She straightened up in the saddle and guided Teasel downhill.

"I'll take you home and get you cooled down and brushed, darling girl, then I'll talk to Headmaster Michael and Jill," she said. "You still need to see Mrs Tilney and she still needs to see you. But I'll tell them that you don't like horseboxes."

Then, having explained everything to Teasel, she saw what she'd been missing. She patted Teasel's neck.

"But it's not up to me, and it's not up to Michael and Jill. It's up to Mrs Tilney! Nobody else can decide what to do with you. It's best if you stay here until she's better, and she'll decide what to do with you. In the meantime, darling girl, I'll look after you, as I told her I would. Doesn't that sound. . ."

She didn't see the grouse as it rose from the moor. She only heard the raucous croak. Teasel's shoulders dropped, and she plunged forward. Gwen lurched forward and fought to stay in the saddle as Teasel swerved wildly round.

"Teasel!" shouted Gwen. The world turned upside down, then black.

*

As Gwen had imagined, it was a while before anybody noticed. Dad had just asked where she was, and Mum was saying that as soon as Gwen got on that horse she was sure to forget all idea of time, when the phone call came.

Chapter Six

Teasel was unhappy, and showed it. She had neighed and whinnied for her friends, but only Hattie came. She no longer chased Hattie away, because who else did she have for comfort? She stood with her ears flattened against her head and the whites of her eyes showing. First Arabella had gone away, and now Gwen did not come to her. There were only those new people, and she had no reason to trust them. They were still strangers. She ate the hay they brought and drank the water, but if they tried to touch her she stamped a hoof and tossed her head. *Go away. I don't want to know you.* And worse was to come.

More strangers had arrived. Now that Mrs Tilney and Gwen had gone, it seemed that anyone could walk into her paddock. And the new strangers had brought something terrible. A prison with a narrow door. It was like a horrible dark tunnel with no escape, and terrible memories stirred in Teasel.

Somebody she didn't know had walked into her field, taken hold of her head collar and clipped on a lead rope. Crying out for Arabella and for Gwen, she had reared up and beat her hooves against the air.

The woman with the lead rope had talked and tried to soothe her, but Teasel didn't want to hear any of it. This woman had tried to tell her she was in charge, but no, no. She would take food from her hand, but she would not follow her into that dark space. How could she, when the very sight of it maddened her? It was no good anybody putting food in there, or making encouraging noises. When she sensed a movement behind her, she kicked.

"If she won't go, she won't," said the woman with the lead rein. "We'll try again tomorrow, when she's had a chance to calm down."

"She needs a bigger trailer," suggested Jill. "Maybe she's claustrophobic, afraid of closed spaces."

Michael, who had just darted away from Teasel's hooves, laughed. "I don't think horses get claustrophobia," he said. "She's just not used to the trailer thing. If we keep showing it to her, she'll settle down, won't you, Teasel?" He tried to pat her neck, but she swung her head away from him.

"We'll see about a bigger trailer," said the woman. "Won't be much different, though. She must have been in one before, surely? How did she get here in the first place?"

Jill and Michael looked at each other.

"I've no idea," said Jill. "Aunt Arabella must know."

"We can't discuss it with her," said Michael. "All she has to know is that everything is all right. I mean, as all right as it needs to be."

"And what about Gwen?" asked Jill. At the sound of Gwen's name, Teasel's ears twitched.

"What about her?" said Michael. "We should leave her to her parents. After a fall like that, she might not be allowed to come back."

"Michael," said Jill. "That's not enough. Gwen still cares about Teasel and Teasel still cares about Gwen. We shouldn't leave her out of this."

While Teasel kicked and glared at the trailer, Gwen was reliving the moment of her fall. The first few seconds as she fell sideways from the saddle were hazy, but the cuts and bruises carried the memory for her. Sometimes, at night, she dreamed of it all – hanging on to the reins, stumbling and scrabbling to get to her feet, Teasel's powerful hoof catching her on the shoulder, falling again, the pain in her wrist, her face hitting gravel. The warm salt taste of blood in her mouth.

She would wake in the morning and sit up slowly, biting her lip against pain and stiffness. She didn't like looking in the mirror. Cuts, bruises and three days of tearful arguments and crying over Teasel had made her eyes red and puffy. Now that the bruises were a few days old they looked worse, not better.

After her fall Teasel had settled down and waited for her, standing patiently while Gwen struggled to her hands and knees. She had run her grazed hands over Teasel's legs to check for injuries, then, with a wince of pain, climbed back into the saddle.

"Walk on," she had said, and in the long plod home she had held the reins gathered in her hands while she clung to the pommel in front of her the way she had taught Jack, to keep herself from falling again. Pain in her wrist, pain in her face, pain in her shoulder, blood on her lip. She had to keep going.

In the paddock, she slipped down from the saddle as cautiously as she could, but still a surge of sickening pain made her head swim. She waited, leaning her head against the hard leather of the saddle until it passed. She told herself, *All I have to do is get her saddle off. Now all I have to do is take off her bridle. Good girl, Teasel. Now check each hoof – now brush her. . .*

She had heard Jill's voice behind her, asking her if she was all right. Then she had turned to her, and seen the shock on her face.

She tried to explain to Michael and Jill, and Mum when she arrived, that lots of people have worse falls, and she didn't think she'd damaged anything. At the hospital her wrist had been X-rayed. The nurses told her it wasn't broken, strapped it up, and sent her home with painkillers.

Falling off Teasel had made her gasp with pain, but

it hadn't made her cry. The tears had begun the next day, in the kitchen. When Charlotte and the boys were out of the way, Mum and Dad sat down at one end of the kitchen table with Gwen at the other. Mum slapped her hand down on the table so that the teapot rattled.

"You could have been killed!" she said. "One kick from those hooves! Never mind your helmet, that only protects your head, and I'm beginning to wonder if there's anything in there! You could have been trampled to death! One kick could have broken your back!"

"Mum, I've ridden her safely for weeks," pleaded Gwen.

"Not galloping over the moors like that, you haven't," said Mum.

"We weren't galloping," said Gwen, but it sounded more like "galloming" because her mouth still hurt. "Teasel just got soo . . . smoo . . . smooked at something!"

"But that's the point," Mum persisted. "She could get spooked anywhere! It was different when you had lessons and all you girls rode out together with a teacher, but not like this, up on the moors at the back end of nowhere on your own."

"Everyone falls off," said Gwen with difficulty. "And I didn't have anyone else to ride with."

That was when Dad had pulled a fistful of tissues out of the box and pushed them across the table to her because he knew she'd need them. Then he laid his big, bony hand over hers, and said, "We're not cross with you, Gwen, we just got a shock. You know what your mum's like. She goes up like a rocket and comes down again. Now, I don't know a thing about horses. I'm just a man who drives trains, and they don't have minds of their own, or at least, they don't kick. So I don't claim to understand anything about horses. All I know is that what happened yesterday mustn't happen again."

"It won't," said Mum. Her voice was gentler now. "Now, Gwen, this won't be easy, but it's for the best. Michael Bailey's been on the phone. When Mrs Tilney comes out of hospital she's to go and live with Michael and Jill, so they're putting Teasel into one of those live-in stables. . ."

"Livery stables?" asked Gwen, and sniffed.

"Near where they live. They're very grateful for all you've done."

"But it's up to Mrs Tilney!" argued Gwen.

"Mrs Tilney isn't well enough to make decisions," said Dad gently.

"Then why can't they wait until she is?" she asked.

Mum sighed as if she'd had more than enough of this. She stood up.

"Gwen, they're her family and we're not," she said. "They've decided what they're going to do, and we – you – have to accept it."

The pricking behind Gwen's eyes and the pain in her throat became unbearable. Hot tears splashed down her face, so that the wad of tissues turned into a soggy mess in her hand. Dad patted her shoulder.

"There's nothing we can do about it, love," he said. "You've done a great job with that pony, but you couldn't go on, all alone, with nobody to help you."

Gwen fought for her voice. She had to get the words out.

"She won't go!"

"She's going, Gwen, that's how it is," said Mum.

Gwen gulped and tried again.

"You're not listening! She won't! They'll never get her into a trailer!"

By the middle of the week, Gwen was back at school during the day and grounded in the evenings. This was supposed to be so that she had time to get better. She suspected that Mum just didn't dare let her out in case she jumped on to Teasel's back, rode away and went to live in a cave somewhere. She was still tired at the end of her first day back at school, and had gone to bed early when Mum came in.

"That's a good idea," said Mum, sitting down on the bed. "You need to rest yourself better. Now listen to this. Jill Bailey just phoned. She said that Teasel's going to a lovely stables called Kennedy Barns, near where they live, and you're very welcome to go and see her any time at weekends or school holidays. You can stay with Michael and Jill. Isn't that kind of them? They're doing their best to keep you involved."

"Yes, I suppose so," admitted Gwen. She wanted to explain that, however kind they were, it would never be Teasel, Mrs Tilney and herself again. She didn't want to seem ungrateful; she simply didn't know how she could bear that. Then Charlotte wandered in without knocking. She had a room of her own, but most of her clothes were in the wardrobe she shared with Gwen. She threw open the door and rattled the coat hangers as she looked about for a top.

"Charlotte, do you have to make such a racket?" said Mum. "And Gwen, Michael Bailey said to ask you about something. Something about a horsebox or a trailer or something. They can't get the pony into it."

Gwen flopped back on to the pillows and shut her eyes. She could have told them that.

"So he said, could you go over at the weekend and help to get her in, because the pony knows you?" asked Mum.

Gwen sat bolt upright again and winced with pain.

"He said what?"

Charlotte glanced over her shoulder.

"Drama queen," she said, and went on clattering coat hangers about.

"He turns up," cried Gwen, "he takes over, he tries to force Teasel into a prison, or at least, something she thinks of as a prison. . ." Charlotte turned round, rolled her eyes, and sighed dramatically, ". . .they want to cart her off for hours and hours in a trailer that she's scared of to a place where she'll be unhappy, and he wants me to help!"

"Oh, rats on a stick!" said Charlotte. "It's just getting a horse in a trailer. You're not herding elephants on to the Ark!"

"Charlotte!" exclaimed Mum, but, as usual, Charlotte was making her laugh. "But she's right, Gwen. The pony has to go whether she likes it or not. We can't always get what we want."

I will murder the next person who says that, thought Gwen. But there was no way of keeping Teasel. This time, not even love, or Gwen, could find a way.

I'm sorry, darling girl. I don't have a choice. If only I did.

For three days Charlotte talked about making ponies into food, then it was Sunday, and Gwen returned to Lady Anne Cottages. She avoided the house. It would always be Mrs Tilney's house to her, a place of worn-out clothes and cheap biscuits. Michael and Jill in there were like pieces of the wrong jigsaw. The Land Rover parked in the lane beside the paddock looked too shabby to be anything to do with Michael and Jill, so that must be from the livery stables at Kennedy Barns.

Gwen went straight to the paddock. The trailer had been left by the gate in the hope that Teasel would get used to it, but Teasel was showing what she thought of it. She stood as far away as possible, with her back to it, near to the fence so that she had Hattie for company. Gwen clicked her tongue and called Teasel's name.

Teasel whirled round and there was a whinny of joy as she cantered to Gwen's side, her mane and tail streaming. She nuzzled at Gwen's jacket, pushed at her pocket and ate a mint messily from her hand.

"Darling girl!" whispered Gwen, nestling her face again Teasel's smooth neck. "My beautiful girl, I've missed you!"

Even ungroomed and with a rug over her golden coat, Teasel was beautiful. Seeing her for the first time in a week, Gwen was struck all over again by her colour, her long Rapunzel mane, and her soft, kind eyes. She was completely lovable. Somebody had already put travelling boots round her legs, ready for going into the trailer. Gwen had hoped to do that herself.

"You bucked me off and kicked me, remember?" said Gwen, stroking her. "No, I'm not here to ride you today. Shall I lead you round a bit?"

"What are you doing in here?" shouted a voice, and Teasel shied away. A big woman in a padded jacket and jeans climbed down from the Land Rover and strode towards them, glaring down at Gwen.

Gwen stared steadily back at her. Charlotte had been winding her up all morning, and she was in no mood for any trouble from anyone else.

"I'm supposed to be here," she said calmly. "Mr and Mrs Bailey sent for me."

"Oh, you must be Jen," said the woman. "Sorry about that. We can't have just anyone wandering in here. I'm Karen, I'm from Kennedy Barns Stables, and I'm here to take Teasel back there."

"It's Gwen," said Gwen, but Karen didn't appear to be listening. Michael and Jill had seen her, and came outside to join them.

"It's very kind of you to come and help us, Gwen," said Jill kindly. Gwen only half smiled. She didn't want to make this easy for them.

"As your mum may have told you, we've been trying to get Teasel into the trailer, but she won't go," said Michael. "We've tried putting food in it, but it's still no good. She backs away, veers to the side or kicks out. Do you think you can work your magic on her?"

Gwen turned away, pressed her face against Teasel's neck and closed her eyes. Did they have any idea what they were asking of her? To take her trusting best friend to a place where she didn't want to be, and abandon her there?

"Gwen?" said Jill.

Gwen raised her head. She couldn't hate Jill, but she turned to Michael with a look of pure loathing.

"She has to go, love," said Karen from behind her. "We'll take good care of her. Can you just help her in? Only we haven't got time to hang around."

Gwen stared coldly into her eyes. "Teasel doesn't understand about your time," she said. "It'll take as long as it takes. I might be able to make her go, but I can't make her like it. Wait a minute, I need a photograph. And some scissors."

She took her phone from her pocket and took three photographs of Teasel, knowing that Karen was looking at her watch and fidgeting with the keys of the Land Rover. Michael asked her what she wanted scissors for, but Jill gave him a stern look, went indoors and brought them from the kitchen. Gwen put them in her pocket. It was time to take control.

"Everybody, stand well back," she ordered, and even Karen shuffled away. "Open all the trailer doors. The side one, too; we need to get as much light in as possible. Is there a hay net in there for her?"

She could see a tightness at the corners of Teasel's mouth. She was already wary, and Gwen didn't take her straight to the trailer. She turned her and led her round the paddock, treasuring every graceful step, every tread of her hooves, talking to distract her from the sound of doors opening and the ramp being pushed into place. Hattie came to the fence and she stopped to pat her rough old neck and talk to her. Then she took a deep breath and tried to relax, because if she got upset, so would Teasel, and Teasel needed to stay as calm as she could for as long as she could. At last, Gwen clicked her tongue.

"Walk on, darling girl," she said, quietly, and walked on to the ramp as if they were still strolling round the paddock. With one hoof on the ramp, Teasel stopped.

"Good girl, walk on." Gwen gave another click and a gentle pull on the halter. "That's it. Darling girl, I know, I know you don't like it, but you'll be fine. Yes. Shh, shh. I'm coming in with you. Gwen's here. You'll be fine." And Teasel followed, as Gwen knew she would.

"There's your hay net," she said, and quickly tethered Teasel to the bar in front so she couldn't escape. "That's my good brave girl. Shh. Shh."

Over the top of Teasel's head, she could see Karen looking at her watch again. Well, Karen would just have to wait. Teasel was throwing her head up and laying her ears flat against her skull. Her tail swished.

"It's going to be fine," whispered Gwen. "They'll look after you, and I'll come to see you. Didn't I promise to take care of you? Be a good girl. Stand. That's it."

Teasel's long, flaxen mane hung to one side. Gwen stroked it, then drew the scissors from her pocket and snipped a few long hairs to keep. There was one last, tight hug, one more chance to press her head against Teasel's neck, then she walked away, not looking back, because she couldn't bear to.

Where is Gwen? Teasel tried to turn and follow her, but she could not turn. Something behind her creaked and clanged, and suddenly the light was dim. She turned her head, one way and the other, and kicked out, testing the space, and knew with a rising terror that she had been shut in the dark. *Let me out! Gwen, Arabella, come for me!* She threw up her head, crying out to Gwen to come for her, to get her out, out of this box. But it was moving! It was rocking her from side to side, dragging her away and there was nothing she could do, nothing. She was helpless, trapped and terrified. She stood still, her ears back, and trembled, crying out for Gwen and Arabella.

Gwen couldn't bear to see the trailer go, or hear Teasel whinnying for her. She walked into the utility room and was grateful to Michael and Jill for leaving her alone, but even there she could hear the clang as Teasel stamped at her prison floor.

The utility room was empty. The stable fork, the hay bales, Teasel's saddle and bridle and her rug had all gone. There were no hoof picks, brushes or sponges. Everything had been swept. There was only Gwen, kneeling on the floor with the scissors besides her and a lock of Teasel's mane in her fingers.

Chapter Seven

I don't like you, I don't want to know you. I don't even want to see you. Don't come near me. I want my people, my Gwen, my friend. Teasel shivered in the trailer. Every change of speed made her throw her head up in fear; every swerve and lurch made her kick. The hay net was no comfort, for she was too anxious to eat. It was all too fast, and whenever she kicked there was a noise and a rattle. By the time the Land Rover halted in the stableyard at Kennedy Barns, she was raging with fear and anger.

A woman in a waxed jacket and jeans had heard them coming. She came out to meet the trailer.

"Bring her out forward, Linda," called Karen, getting out of the Land Rover. "Give her time. She's got a temper on her."

Teasel stood at the open door of the trailer and glared out at a hard grey yard. There were buildings on all sides of her, making a memory of fear flick into her mind. She stood still, twitching her ears and listening. Nothing about this place was good. She liked grass, not a yard, and moorland, not prison cells. She wanted her own paddock, with Hattie, Arabella and Gwen, and neighed for them.

"Everyone stand back," said Linda. "Teasel, it's all right. Good girl."

But as Linda took the lead rope, Teasel planted her feet down firmly and flattened her ears back. The trailer had been bad, but whatever was outside might be worse. There were human voices around and the neighing and whinnying of horses, but they were strangers. She stamped, tossed her head, and pawed with her hoof. She would not do anything for these people.

Linda made soothing noises. "Teasel, walk on," she said.

Linda's voice was a little like Mrs Tilney's, and Teasel was used to obeying that command, but fear and anger held her fast. A gentle tug at the lead rope made her resist and shake her head, showing the whites of her eyes.

"This is going to take time," observed Karen. "We've got a right one here."

Finally, it was only thirst that made Teasel walk down the ramp and out of the trailer. The people had left a bucket of water in the yard, and when she had to, she drank. After that she allowed them to walk her round the stableyard, but only in the hope of finding somebody she knew, neighing out to them. *Arabella, where are you? Why did you leave me? Gwen, where have you gone? Why did you leave me in the box? Where is Hattie? Where are my friends? Where is the fresh grass that tastes of home?*

"I'll turn her out in a paddock," said Linda. "They said she doesn't like being inside, and she's stressed enough without that."

"She'll get picked on by the others," said Karen, leading a reluctant Teasel round the yard.

"She'll go in the small field by herself to start with," answered Linda. "She might be lonely, but she won't get bitten."

So Teasel grazed alone in the field, where the grass was sweet. They let her stay outside, and slowly she became calmer. But this was not her place. Where was Gwen? People came to talk to her and brush her. She was fed. But night fell, day came, and there was no Gwen and no Arabella.

"This weekend," said Gwen. "*Please?* Can I go to see her this weekend?"

"Give her a bit longer to settle in," suggested Mum. "Next weekend will be better. That's when Dad's got a long weekend off, so he can take you there the minute you get out of school. We might be able to book some riding lessons next term. Jill says Teasel's settling in."

"But Jill would say that," Gwen pointed out.

"There's no need for that attitude," said Mum firmly. "It's only one week to wait. And in the meantime, you could go to the hospital and see how Mrs Tilney's getting on."

So Gwen found the diary that had been a free gift with one of her pony magazines and ticked off the days one by one, but every day was too long. She drew sketches of Teasel, trying and failing to capture the pretty dished curve of her face, and pinned her photographs of Teasel over the desk. Then she printed out another set of those photos, and took them with her when she visited Mrs Tilney.

There was an unpleasant smell about the hospital, and Gwen wrinkled up her nose. It was something like a blend of sick and disinfectant, but she had to be there, and she found her way through long white corridors and up the stairs to Ward Five. As well as her pictures of Teasel, she had brought biscuits and bananas for Mrs Tilney.

There were three rooms in the ward, and each had rows of beds with identical green and white covers. Gwen, looking in at the door, had no idea how to find Mrs Tilney. She couldn't very well walk round looking at all the patients – it would be like going round the zoo and gawping at the animals. By the door a sunken-cheeked woman lay propped up on white pillows, snoring gently.

"Can I help?" asked a nurse. "Are you looking for someone?"

"Arabella Tilney, please," said Gwen.

"Arabella Tilney?" repeated the nurse. "Yes, she's just here. You'll find her speech is slurred, and she sometimes mixes up her words and gets things back to front. That's normal after a stroke. She will improve, but you have to listen to her carefully. She's dozing a bit, but I'll just check if she's anywhere near the surface."

She bent over the woman snoring on the pillows. The eyes flickered open.

"Arabella?" said the nurse loudly. "There's a young lady here to see you."

It might have been embarrassment, or maybe it was the overheated ward, but Gwen turned hot and cold. She hadn't recognized Mrs Tilney! The shrivelled woman in the cotton nightie, her head drooping and a little dribble coming from the corner of her mouth, the woman with arms as creased as crepe paper – surely that wasn't Arabella Tilney?

The blue eyes opened. To Gwen's delight, they turned to her and the light of mischief sparkled into them. Gwen relaxed. Mrs Tilney might look much older, but the brightness was still there.

"How are you feeling, Arabella?" asked the nurse loudly.

"I ee . . . I . . . eef, eash, ursh," said Mrs Tilney from the only corner of her mouth that worked. Gwen had to work out what this meant, but when she realized that it was, "I need my teeth, please, nurse," she turned her head away and pretended to be very interested in the curtains. When she looked back, Mrs Tilney looked a lot more like her usual self. Her face was still lopsided and she looked older than ever, but at least she had her teeth in.

"How dolly nishe of you to come and shee me!" she exclaimed, and heaved herself a little more upright. Gwen reached an arm round her to help her, and the nurse plumped up the pillows. Even speaking from only one side of her mouth, Mrs Tilney still sounded like an old duchess.

"Gosh, danksh awfy, Gen!" she exclaimed when she saw the fruit and biscuits. "How'sh my shmashing girl?"

"Jill says she's fine," said Gwen, seating herself down beside the bed. She had to be careful because if they talked a lot about Teasel, Mrs Tilney might get upset. "I'm going to see her at the weekend."

Mrs Tilney frowned. "I meant you, shilly," she said.

"Oh!" Gwen gave a little smile and a shrug. "I'm OK. How are you doing?"

"Tired and shick of being ill," growled Mrs Tilney, then she asked about Teasel, and Gwen found that she could talk about her without either of them crying. She decided that Mrs Tilney didn't have to know how distressed Teasel had been about the trailer.

"Jill says she's settling down at Kennedy Barns," she said.

"Dey should never haff taken her," said Mrs Tilney grumpily. "She wash fine where she wash. Dere are perfectly shtablesh good – oh, bovver, good shtablesh – 'ound here. Dill'sh an awfy nishe girl, but she doeshn't know a fing about horshesh."

Mum had warned Gwen not to stay too long – "no more than fifteen minutes, because she'll get tired" – but every time Gwen tried to get away, Mrs Tilney held her hand more tightly and started telling yet another story about Teasel, or some other horse she had owned when she was young, or the bears that would raid their rubbish bins when she and Jeremy had lived in Canada, or mad dogs in Africa. At one point, Gwen looked up at the ward clock and began to say, "I really should go now," but Mrs Tilney followed her glance.

"Shicsh clock," she said. "Time for the newsh." She picked up a remote control unit from the bed table and stabbed it awkwardly at the small television at the end of the bed.

"Michael shorted thish thing out for me," she said. "Can't get the 'etched thing going. You aff a go. And turn down the . . . noishe . . . talker . . . shound."

Gwen didn't know why Mrs Tilney wanted the television on as she had the sound turned down and kept talking, but her eyes strayed now and again to the screen. Gwen, knowing that it's very hard to ignore a television when it's on, turned her back on it and made a determined effort to concentrate on Mrs Tilney instead.

"Mum and Dad said I can go riding again in the summer," she said, to keep the conversation going. "They said I can have some more lessons." Should she go on and talk about Charlotte's grade seven violin exam? Jack and Robin wanting to learn the trombone?

But increasingly Mrs Tilney looked more interested in the news than in anything she said, so this might be a good time to leave. She was trying to find the right way of saying goodbye when Mrs Tilney sat bolt upright in bed and pointed at the screen.

"Eashel!" she cried out. "Ook! Gwen! It'sh Eashel!"

Gwen turned to look at the television and saw a grey, blurred film, the kind that comes from security cameras. A pony was galloping away from a petrol station, its tail flying and its heels lifting as it cleared a fence. It was only for a second or two, but Gwen knew Teasel's shape and the way she moved. A big, round-faced man appeared on the screen.

"I was just serving a customer when somebody came running in to say there was a loose horse around, and then we all heard the hooves," he said. "I ran outside and there was this horse belting across the forecourt. It nearly hit a car. There could have been an accident."

"Did you try to catch the horse?" asked the interviewer.

"No way," said the man. "There was no getting near it. It had no reins, nor anything on it, nothing you could grab hold of. I was dead scared it would get on to the dual carriageway and there'd be a pile-up, but it made for the hedge and jumped over. Don't know where it went after that."

Mrs Tilney was leaning forward as if she wanted to climb into the screen. "It's Eashel!" she shouted. "Gwen, find out what'sh happening!"

Teasel had waited very patiently for Arabella and Gwen, but they still hadn't come. Slowly, she had come to understand that this was not their place. It was Linda's place, and she was the one to be friends with. Linda had led her into the field with the other horses and she was the newest and least important horse there, but so long as she remembered it and stayed in her place they didn't chase or bite her. When she was young she had lived on the hill, so she knew how to behave. At least, so far, nobody had tried to put her in a box again. *I don't belong in a box, and I hate to be forced. If you force me, I will fight. I belong in the sun and rain and the open air, and you cannot take them from me. Nobody will take them from me again.*

Being kept in her place was normal, but those hideous box things were not. Those were evil traps that swallowed you, rattled you, and took you to strange places against your will. No, never ever again.

When Linda put her on a long rein and asked her to trot round in circles, she knew what to do. She had been trained this way, and enjoyed it, holding up her head and showing off her stride. There was sugar at the end of it, too. She enjoyed being praised, and the day came when she let Linda ride her round the yard. Linda wasn't as light as Gwen, but she was comfortable to carry, and sat easily. The day would have ended calmly and happily if not for the noise of an engine.

Teasel heard it while Linda was grooming her, as Gwen used to groom her. There was a rumble and roar, the noise that meant the boxes were coming! And it was louder, and louder! She laid back her ears and stamped in fear and anger.

"Steady, Teasel!" said Linda, patting her gently. "Karen, she's spooking about something. Will you turn her out?"

Karen led her to the field, but Teasel shied and shook her head all the way there, only standing still while Karen slipped off her head collar. But even in the field, she could still hear them. They were coming for her.

When the Land Rover brought the empty trailer clanging and clattering into the yard, Linda understood what had spooked Teasel, and what was making the other horses canter away over the field. She ran across the yard.

"What do you think you're doing?" she yelled. "You're terrifying the—"

The car and trailer lurched to a halt with a screech of brakes. Doors banged. Terror made Teasel's heart beat hard and fast. The sights and sounds around her filled her with fear. The instincts of generations of horses before her tumbled into her head, all saying, *Run! Get out! Run and keep running!*

She whisked round, galloped, cleared the fence and kept on, trampling the meadow, splashing up mud around her, passing cottages and farm buildings, hurtling forward to put all the distance she could between herself and that terrible box. The sudden freedom told her that nothing was beyond her, she could go anywhere, but then she was on hard ground, with the grim smell and noise of engines around her. A fence – there was a fence. She cleared it, and kept running.

Soon she was among trees. It was an unfamiliar place, but she was sheltered, and they wouldn't find her here. She got her breath back and walked, seeking water. But she was alone again, and alone was not good.

Gwen ran down the stairs and out to the car park. With her hands shaking as she held the phone, she called Michael. Yes, he said calmly, Linda from Kennedy Barns had called him. Teasel had bolted. Nothing to worry about, nothing to panic over.

"Nothing to worry about!" repeated Gwen furiously. "She could be killed on the road! There could be a pile-up!"

"She's not on the road now," said Michael, and his calmness made her furious. "Take a deep breath, Gwen. There are people out looking for her. They'll soon have her back safe and sound. It's best not to say anything to Auntie – we don't want to upset her."

"It's too late for that," she snapped. "She's just seen Teasel on television."

She switched off the phone and marched back into the hospital entrance. *Nothing to worry about.* Just a loose, terrified horse galloping about the countryside. It was a miracle she hadn't been killed, or caused a major traffic accident. *It's no good Michael telling me that everything's under control. It really isn't.*

She imagined Teasel stepping into a ditch and being lamed, with nobody to find her or help her. The idea made her stomach churn and clench. Teasel getting into a field and gorging herself on grain or sweet grass until she was bloated and dying of colic. Teasel caught by someone who would hurt her. *Stop it*, she told herself as she ran up the stairs to the ward. *This isn't helping*.

She found Mrs Tilney sitting up in bed, watching for her with fear and anxiety in her eyes, and the sight of her helped Gwen to be calm. However angry she felt with Michael – and the people at Kennedy Barns, come to that – she had to make this as easy for Mrs Tilney as possible. She took her hand.

"Yes, it was Teasel," she said gently, "but everyone's out looking for her. We'll find her."

Mrs Tilney squeezed her hand. "Oo go," she said. Her speech might be slurred, but the pleading in her eyes was unmistakeable.

"Yes, I'll go," said Gwen. "I don't know how I'm going to get out of school, but I'll find a way."

Mrs Tilney frowned in concentration. "Take mintsh," she said.

In spite of everything, Gwen laughed.

"Yes, I'll take mints," she said.

Even after the long journey home, Gwen was still upset enough to be angry. She banged the door behind her and kicked her shoes at the wall. Jack and Robin, who were playing on the landing, peered through the banisters to see what would happen next. Normally when they did that they looked funny, like monkeys in a cage, but nothing was funny now.

"Gwen, come in and sit down," said Mum, appearing from the sitting room. From her voice, and the fact that she hadn't told her off for slamming the door, Gwen knew what she had to say.

"Mum, if you're going to tell me about Teasel running away, I already know," she said. "It was on Mrs Tilney's hospital telly, so she knows as well." She threw her jacket at a peg, missed, and suddenly, as she bent to pick it up, felt a wave of fear that made her legs weaken and her stomach turn over. "Is there any more news? Has there been. . ." She couldn't quite say "an accident".

"All I know is that the police are out trying to find her," said Mum. "Now, there's not a thing we can do about it, so you'll just have to let Michael and Jill sort it out, and the people at the stables she went to. It's up to them."

"Those stables? What use are they?" demanded Gwen. "They must be a lot of chocolate teapots to let her run away in the first place, and they still haven't got her back! And Michael doesn't know what he's doing! He sent her to a place where they couldn't keep her in and now they can't find her!"

There were tears in her eyes as she ran upstairs, but before she reached her room she knew that she had to do something more useful than curl up and cry. Mum had said that there wasn't a thing they could do about it, but to Gwen, that made no sense. She had promises to keep. She was about to phone Michael again when Jack ran into the room.

"Mum says to come to the phone," he said. He grabbed her hand and dragged her excitedly from the room. "It's about your Teasel. You have to find her. I can help, if you like."

Teasel sheltered in the dappled shade of the forest, but soon she would move on again. Food and water were easy to find, and her early years on the hill had made her hardy. The fresh, outside air was good. She missed company, but she would not be caught. Nobody would put her in a box and rattle her about again.

An engine growled near to her, and somebody got out of a car. A man was pointing something at her – a stick? She ducked and swerved as something flew past her ear, and breaking into a gallop, she escaped. All those rides with Gwen had made her strong and fast, and now, with nobody to carry, she felt airborne. If she could, she would have laughed.

She needed the company of other horses. It wasn't safe to be alone, so she must find friends, but there was nobody to help her find them. She must rely on her own courage, her speed, her wits, and the instincts of the hill pony. As she cantered away she kept her ears pricked, listening for whinnies. Somewhere, there must be a herd that would let her in. In the meantime, if any people came for her, she could outrun them easily.

At first she followed the bridlepaths, because she had travelled paths like this with Gwen, but the first time she saw a horse coming towards her she turned and bolted across an open meadow. The horse might be a friend, but the rider could not be trusted, so she ran until she was under cover again. Instinct told her to take rocky ground, humpy and hummocky, difficult ground, too hard for people to follow her with their rattling crates. When she felt safe, she pulled up a mouthful of grass.

The grass was good, and different from the taste of her own paddock. There was something familiar about it – at some time in her life, she must have tasted grass like this. She grazed, wanting more, then went on her way slowly, hearing no human voices, but only birdsong and the chattering of a stream.

She knew she must not be alone. It wasn't safe to live like that. She needed company. But she had learned to be wary. She would choose her own friends.

Gwen sat on the stairs with the phone in her hand and listened to Michael.

"I don't normally approve of pupils having time off in term time," he said, rather pompously.

Gwen could picture him saying it. *I bet you don't*, she thought, crossing her eyes and sticking her tongue out at the phone, *but it's not all about you*. She put the phone to her ear again.

"However, the pony is a danger to the public and the police are involved, so if there's any chance that you can catch her, you need to be here. I'm going to phone your headteacher before school in the morning and arrange for you to have the day off."

"Thank you!" said Gwen automatically. What else would she say to a headmaster who'd just given her a day off school? But she wasn't thinking "thank you". He was still trying to organize everything, including her, but at least he was doing something sensible this time. He was still talking.

"Now, Jill and I are both working all day tomorrow," he went on. "But our daughter Lily is home from university just now, so she'll come and pick you up and bring you here. It'll be best if you stay over the weekend with us, and talk to the local police, and between us we'll get Teasel rounded up."

"But nobody even knows where she is," Gwen pointed out. "She could be anywhere!"

"Yes, well, we'll see what we can do," said Michael airily. "I'm sure the police will do a great job. Bring some photos of the horse, will you? Any other questions?"

Any other questions? thought Gwen, as if she'd received the end of her marching orders. *Were you in the army?*

"Yes," she said. "If we do find her and catch her, what will happen to her next? Where will she go?"

"We'll sort that out when we come to it, shall we?" suggested Michael. "To begin with, let's just get her back." And he had gone before she could ask anything else. Heaven alone knew what "our daughter Lily" would be like.

She put down the phone and wandered into the sitting room where her parents and Charlotte were watching the news. Charlotte was eating a yoghurt and didn't look up when Gwen came in.

"Michael's getting me the day off tomorrow to look for Teasel," she said. "I'm getting picked up—" but she stopped when the newsreader said, "And finally, to the pony who's becoming famous as Tearaway Teasel since she escaped and headed for the wild. She was sighted this afternoon near Mold on the Welsh borders. CCTV cameras found her here. . . ." They showed another grainy, jerky bit of film. "But she's doing very well at avoiding capture and has dodged attempts to sedate her with tranquillizer darts."

"*What!*" snapped Gwen.

The newsreader went on. "Staff at the Kennedy Barns Equestrian Centre were not available for comment. So tonight, Tearaway Teasel is still on the run."

Charlotte finally looked up. "Teasel?" she said. "Isn't that your mad old lady's horse? What have you done now?"

"Charlotte!" said Mum and Dad together. Gwen stared with wide eyes. Nobody ever spoke to Charlotte like that.

Chapter Eight

"Er . . . hello?" asked Gwen as she opened the door. "Are you one of Charlotte's friends?"

The girl on the doorstep made everything around her look dull. Her smile was so bright and friendly, with her lips so covered in deep-red lipstick, that it was impossible not to smile back. Under huge eyelashes her eyes had a twinkle of mischief that reminded Gwen of Mrs Tilney. Her hair was so blonde it was almost white, with pink tips, and earrings glittered through it. She wore a short, frothy pink dress over green leggings, and her clumpy red boots were laced to the ankles. Bracelets glittered on one arm, a tiny butterfly was tattooed on the opposite wrist, and her fingernails were sparkling scarlet. She carried car keys.

"Who's Charlotte?" she asked, still smiling. "I'm Lily Bailey. Are you Gwen?"

Gwen tried to stop staring. She failed. She couldn't help it.

"Are you Michael and Jill's daughter?" she faltered.

Lily laughed a loud, cackling laugh. "Yeah, it's a surprise, isn't it?" she said. "I've come to take you on a pony hunt. You ready to go?" Then she glanced past Gwen to the hall and gave a little fingertip wave.

Gwen turned. Her whole family stood speechless at the kitchen door. Jack and Robin's mouths hung open. Mum and Dad looked stunned. Gwen could almost hear the wheels turning in Mum's head as she tried to think of a good reason to stop her from going. Charlotte, who looked as if she was staring at a goddess, spoke first.

"Hi, I'm Charlotte," she said. "I love your hair!"

"Cool, thanks!" said Lily.

"I've packed a bag," said Gwen, and picked it up from its place by the door before anyone could try to make her stay. "Bye, see you soon!"

"Don't worry, I'll take care of her – we won't crash!" called Lily cheerfully. "I'm a good driver!" As they walked down the path, Gwen heard Charlotte say, "Is our Gwen going with *her*?"

In the car, Lily took a jacket from the passenger seat and threw it into the back so that Gwen could sit beside her. Then she flicked her phone on.

"OK, Gal, we'll get going in a minute," she said.

"Gal's the car, by the way." She spoke into the phone. "Hi, Mum! Yeah, I've just got her. Any more sightings of the pony? Cool. Where, Mum? Talleravon? Well, there's no point in coming home if she was last seen in Talleravon, is there? See you later, Mum!" She closed the phone, grinned at Gwen and turned the key in the ignition. "OK, sweetie? Hope you don't mind sweetie – I call everyone that. Even Dad. Smile, we're going to find your pony!"

Gwen used to think that Charlotte was the most confident person she knew, but Lily was from another world. Chatting, driving, laughing, asking about Teasel, singing with the music in the car, she was awe-inspiring. By the time they found the village of Talleravon, Gwen's stomach was beginning to ache with hunger, but just as she wondered whether Lily ever needed to eat, there was a call from the driving seat – "I'm starving, are you? Look out for a car park!"

"On the right, next turning!" said Gwen.

"Cool," said Lily. She parked the car and, with a flutter of earrings, jerked her head towards a prettily painted coffee shop. "There's a cafe over there. Looks OK."

Gwen's parents had given her money for this trip and she took out her purse, but Lily waved her hand. "Put that away," she said. "Mum and Dad gave me the money for this. It's cool."

When they got into the cafe, Gwen was even more impressed by Lily. Looking at the menu, she didn't like to order much – she'd hate Lily to think she was greedy – but Lily took charge. Before long, she seemed to have taken over the whole cafe.

"Is that all you're having?" she asked. "You need to eat more than that, sweetie – it'll be a long day and I don't want you fainting on me. Have some chips with it. If you don't eat them, I will. Have you got your pictures of the pony?"

Gwen had brought the photos of Teasel that she usually kept pinned above her desk. She passed them across the table. Lily picked them up, and her eyes widened.

"Oh, isn't she gorgeous?" she exclaimed. "Bless! What a colour! Oh, just look at that pretty face!" She was still sifting through them when the waitress came to take their order.

"Bacon and brie baguette for me, cheese salad and chips for Gwen," she said. "And have you seen this pony?"

Her loud, clear voice filled the room. Customers heads turned. Gwen's face felt hot.

"Oh, now, isn't that the runaway pony?" said the waitress. "The one they call Tearaway Teasel?"

"Yeah, that's her," said Lily. She stood up, a photograph in her hand, holding it up to left and right and raising her voice. "Has anyone seen her? Anyone?"

Around them, people shook their heads or pretended to be very interested in their salads, or reading the newspapers, or deaf. Gwen nearly did the same – but if being loud and pestering people would help to find Teasel, that's what she'd have to do. She picked up a picture. It was the last one she'd taken, just before Teasel was shut away in the horsebox. She was still looking down at it, with a sharp pang of pain in her heart, when Lily snatched it from her fingers.

"Here," said Lily, showing it to the manageress, who had come to see what the fuss was about. "That's her. Isn't she beautiful?" She gave the picture back to Gwen. "Will you ask the kitchen staff, please? Thanks so much. Thank you. You're a star."

"Chips look good," remarked Lily, when the food arrived. "Enjoy."

They were halfway through their meal when a customer from another table came to join them. She carried an iPhone in her hand.

"I just checked out the news sites for that pony," she said. "She's been seen on the Welsh side of the border, near Llan – you say that sort of 'Thlan', don't you? – something or other. Hang on . . . Llanabos."

"Thank you!" said Gwen. Hope made her feel lighter already.

"Wow, thanks!" said Lily. "How do you spell that?"

In a flourishing italic script, she wrote "Llanabos" on a paper napkin. With a few lines, she drew a pony underneath it.

"Now we're on it," she said, and grinned across the table at Gwen. "OK, let's get lunch down and we're off to Thlanny-bo-bo. Keep your eyes open."

They drove through villages, into hills and on to rough, single-track roads where Gal rocked and jiggled. Lily talked to her the way Gwen talked to Teasel, like an equal. At farm gates, they would stop so that Gwen could get out and look for any signs of hoofprints, and call Teasel's name. When they reached a hilltop where a few horses grazed in a field, Lily parked in a layby.

"You've got a good viewpoint here," she said. "Want to get out and have a look?"

Gwen stood on tiptoe at the gate, the wind flicking her hair across her face. She called Teasel's name and heard the sound disappear into the wind. *Come to me, Teasel*, she thought. Her heart reached out as if she could call through earth and sky to Teasel, and her beautiful, golden Teasel would hear her, whinny, and come trotting over the hill to meet her. But there was only the clouded, windy sky, with the horses in the field standing hoof-tilted, or pulling up mouthfuls of grass. When their curiosity brought them to the gate Gwen patted their necks and flapped the flies away from their eyes.

"Hey, you're really great around horses," said Lily, and Gwen felt a blush rise to her forehead. She wouldn't have thought she could impress someone like Lily.

"I've always loved them," she said. "Teasel was all I ever wanted. And when I found her we understood each other – we just enjoyed being together." *Oh, no, I shouldn't have said that. I mustn't cry.* She hugged the nearest horse, and pressed her face against its neck until she wasn't in danger of showing any tears.

"You OK, sweetie?" said Lily. "There's a sign ahead to one of those touristy country park places. You know, national park or forestry or something, where they have car parks and picnic tables and marked footpaths and all that stuff. We'll try there."

This time, they parked in a sheltered car park surrounded by maps giving details of country walks and a lot of instructions about not lighting fires, dropping litter or damaging trees. A signpost led to a five-mile circular walk.

"It goes uphill," said Lily. "There should be a good viewpoint from up there – we might see her." But Gwen couldn't help looking doubtfully at Lily's red boots.

"You don't have to come with me," she said. "I can do the walk on my own, if you'd rather stay in the car and read or something."

"It's cool," said Lily. She pushed the boot open, threw out a pair of wellies painted with bright green grass and daisies, and stepped into them. They were struggling up a hill when Gwen said shyly, "It's really lovely of you to do all this. You don't have to. I mean, I'm taking up so much of your time and there must be things you want to do."

Lily laughed. "No worries!" she said. "I need something to keep me busy. They give you long holidays at uni. I've got a bit of work coming up later – I'm doing a play scheme with kids in an art gallery, but there's nothing happening just now. Except, I mean, I'm still painting and stuff. But this is cool."

That confirmed it. Gwen had guessed that Lily must be an art student. Soon she was talking about silk painting, and the difficulty of getting purple dye off your fingers. She was telling Gwen about her end-of-term exhibition when they reached the top of a hill and stopped to get their breath back while they scanned the view for any sign of ponies. Now that they were high up, the breeze was brisk and Gwen had to hold her hair back from her face with both hands. It reminded her of the day when she had ridden Teasel on the moors and looked down at a toy town. But there was no town here, only the forest giving way to green hills and meadows, a silver stream, and. . .

"Teasel!" she cried, and her heart lurched.

It couldn't be. But it was.

"Teasel!" she said again, and pointed. "Lily, that's her!"

Teasel was so far away that it might have been any palomino pony cantering across a meadow, but Gwen knew her. She knew Teasel's look, her silhouette and her way of moving.

"Where?" asked Lily. She bent to squint along Gwen's outstretched arm, but soon Teasel was out of sight.

"Are you sure that was her?" asked Lily.

"Absolutely sure," said Gwen. "I couldn't mistake her – it's like seeing one of my own brothers or my sister at a distance."

"Fair enough," said Lily. "I can go with that. Let's get back in the car – which way did she go?"

For the rest of that afternoon they drove up and down the narrow roads, walked footpaths, and climbed hills to get another view. There was always the chance that this one last path, just this last turning, would find her. But all the rest of that day there was no more sign of Teasel. By the time they gave up, Gwen's legs ached and her heart had grown dull with disappointment.

"Hey, don't beat yourself up," said Lily as they got into the car. "You've done well. You saw her, didn't you? Did she look OK to you?"

"Yes," said Gwen, and smiled, feeding her heart on that one glimpse of Teasel. "Yes, she looked fine."

Teasel had been well. That was a healthy canter, with no lameness. It was frustrating to have seen her and lost her again, but at least she had seen her, and now she knew that Teasel wasn't hurt.

The journey to the Baileys' house took them to a modern estate where all the houses were different, but they each had big sunny windows and neat front lawns. Lily parked outside one of the largest and prettiest, but by that time Gwen was almost too tired to get out. Her feet hurt as she walked up the path. Michael and Jill must have heard the car arriving, because they were standing at the front door to meet them.

"Hello, Gwen!" said Michael. "Any sightings? Phone your parents so they know you're safe."

"Michael!" said Jill. "Give her a chance! Come in, Gwen. Kick your shoes off if you want. You look exhausted. We'll have dinner on the table soon – you must be starving." She hugged Lily. "Hello, darling!"

Gwen tried to imagine Mum greeting her like that. *Hello, darling!* No, it didn't work. When they sat down at the table Gwen was almost too tired to eat, and felt out of place in the tidy, spacious house. But Lily sat opposite her like a bright rag doll in an empty room, bringing happiness with her. When they had talked for what seemed like hours about the day's progress and the one glimpse of Teasel, Jill offered Gwen a hot drink.

"Will it be all right if I go to bed now?" she asked shyly. She was bitterly tired, and feeling so out of place made it worse.

"Of course. You must be exhausted," said Jill kindly. "We've kept you talking far too long. Now, you just sleep as late as you like in the morning."

Alone in the bedroom, Gwen turned slowly round and round. Now that there was no need to worry about best behaviour, the tension drifted away from her. She began to enjoy being here. A white bed waited for her with its soft cloud of duvet, and a fluffy white rug lay beside it. Mauve towels lay folded on the bed, and the room had its own washbasin! Gwen looked down from the window. A garden with steps and a pond, pretty as a storybook picture, lay below her.

Turning away, she found she was looking at herself in a mirror that took up most of one wall. In a T-shirt and jeans with her messy hair and tired face, she was the one scruffy thing in the perfect bedroom.

She had left her shoes at the front door. Now, she pulled off her socks and sank her tired feet into the softness of the rug. She was about to flop on to the bed when somebody tapped at the door.

"Can I come in?" asked Lily, and slipped into the room. She put a glass of apple juice on the bedside table.

"Forgot to say, you can use my shower if you want," said Lily, and sat down on the floor. "That's my room across the landing with the red poppy on the door. I brought you some apple juice – it's well nice. And I thought you might be homesick."

Gwen laughed. "You don't know much about my home," she said. "It's so different here."

"How do you mean?" asked Lily.

"Well, for a start, your house is quiet," said Gwen.

"Yeah, that's the trouble," said Lily.

"No, it's nice," said Gwen. "Your house is lovely. It felt strange when I first came in. It was . . . I felt like I was a character in the wrong movie. I still do, a bit. But it's so – I don't know – peaceful. In our house there's always stuff lying around everywhere – the twins' toys and everybody's school stuff, and baskets of ironing. There's always washing hanging up somewhere. And it's noisy. So being here, it's lovely, but it's strange. I sort of don't know what to do."

Lily squeezed her hand. "Just be yourself, sweetie!" she assured her. "Don't worry about it. I know what you mean – it's like everybody's on display in this house. But it's good to have somebody different around. I wish I wasn't an only one. I always had to be the Perfect Child. I wish I had a family like yours."

"You don't," said Gwen. "Trust me, you'd hate it. It's all right for Charlotte – she's the star. And everyone thinks the twins are cute, so they get away with murder. I'm just left to get on with things."

"Don't be silly!" said Lily. "They care loads about you! I saw the look on your mum's face when we were leaving – she didn't want you to go in case I wrapped the car round a tree. Now sleep well. Pony hunt again tomorrow."

"Yeah," said Gwen. "Tomorrow we'll find her."

In her dreams that night, Gwen rode mile after mile on Teasel, but then she was standing alone on a hill and Teasel had run away. She woke in the unfamiliar bed, listened to the quiet, and found herself dreaming again. The next day, there was another long, long drive, stopping and starting, asking questions, looking into fields, walking through forests, and seeing ponies that weren't Teasel. For the rest of that weekend, Gwen only saw Teasel in her dreams.

"You're putting yourself out so much to help me find her," said Gwen. She'd never met anyone like Lily. "Why are you doing this?"

Lily only laughed. "Why not?" she said.

In the evening, sitting at the table after dinner, Gwen worked her way through her homework. Jill had told her to ask if she needed help, but she'd said it very kindly and didn't try to take over. Gwen had nearly finished the maths when Lily put a drawing on the table.

"Put that on your wall when you go home," she said.

It was a sketch of Teasel, drawn from one of the

photographs. The pretty curve of her face was perfectly captured, and the shape of her back. Lily had caught the spirit of Teasel so vividly that Gwen's heart leapt.

"I've been trying to do that!" she cried. "I've tried and tried to draw her and I can't get her right. She always looks wooden. I wish I could draw."

"Everyone can draw," said Lily promptly. She pushed the homework books to one side, and Jill gave her a very teacher-ish look.

"OK, finish that first and then I'll show you," she said. By the time Gwen finished the homework, Lily had gathered pencils and torn some blank pages from a sketchbook. They sat side by side drawing, with Lily saying things like "Look at that shape", "Follow the line", and "Look at the shade. . .", until suddenly an hour had passed, leaving Gwen with a far better picture of Teasel than she'd ever drawn before. It wasn't anything like as good as Lily's, but Lily was an art student. She smiled down at it.

"I didn't know I could do that," she said.

"That can go on your bedroom wall," said Lily. "And you'll have the real thing back soon."

The following weekend they tried again, and again there was no trace of Teasel. This time, there were no more reports of her. Nobody had seen her. Using Lily's laptop, they made a poster with a picture of Teasel and Lily's mobile number, and by Sunday night it was in every shop window in three villages, tied to lampposts, and posted up in bus shelters. She spoke to her family on the phone and Jack asked for a poster to take to school for show-and-tell. Gwen knew that it wouldn't do any good, because Teasel was nowhere near home, but it would make Jack feel he was being helpful. Teasel's picture was shared on Lily's Facebook page. But still Teasel was not found.

"There's no more we can do," said Michael on Saturday evening. "She's completely disappeared."

"She's out there somewhere," said Gwen stubbornly. "And I'll find her."

At Kennedy Barns Stables on Sunday she asked for Teasel's tack and sat outside in the sun, cleaning and polishing it for the time when Teasel would need it again. There was to be one more visit to Michael and Jill, then the summer holidays would begin, and Lily would be working in an art gallery. Every night Gwen slept with the strands of Teasel's mane under her pillow, and Lily's sketch and her own on the wall.

There was hope. There was always hope. *Love will find a way*, thought Gwen, as she drifted to sleep.

Chapter Nine

The morning sun woke Teasel. She snorted, shook her head, and began another day of walking, keeping away from houses. She was wary of paddocks where other horses grazed, too. Those were the places where people would come up to her and offer her an apple, but only because they wanted to slip a collar over her head and lead her away. Let them try! She was learning to look after herself. She knew how to rear and kick, leap fences and gallop away. Who could stop her?

The more she travelled, the more she knew which way she must go. The travelling could be hard. The ground was steep and rocky and the mist made her damp, but she was drawn upwards and westwards to the hills. It was her true direction, in her blood and in the instincts and memories she had inherited from her ancestors, so she followed on, eating and drinking where she wanted to. The grass was good, the water was clean and sweet, and they stirred old memories in her. She knew these tastes. She learned to hide among trees, move in early morning and twilight, and outrun anyone who saw her. She went on, further west and further up, until the misty dawn when she arrived at the ancient place where ponies had always lived.

She tore up a few mouthfuls of coarse grass, then raised her head to listen. Somewhere, in the mist, a pony had whinnied. Teasel finished eating and explored a little further. Between clumps and spinneys of trees the turf was rough, but it was springy, too, and felt kind. There were mounds of grass, and little trickling streams that murmured and sparkled as the early light filtered through. Under a silver birch tree, a pony grazed with her dappled foal lying beside her, its head up and one slender foreleg stretched out. Everything about this place was beautiful to Teasel. Above her, birds sang. The feel of the turf stirred memories.

Had the ponies noticed her? Were they ignoring her on purpose, to show that they weren't interested in her?

A roe deer wandered past. It stopped to look steadily at Teasel, then walked away. Teasel stayed, watching the scene without entering it. She might need permission. Another pony came down to graze, and another, not even glancing at her. She couldn't tell whether or not they had seen her.

A brook running just in front of her feet formed a natural barrier, so for now she stayed on her own side of it. The young mare guarded her foal, groomed him, fed and nuzzled him. Mother and Child, Teasel named them. The first pony to come down the hill was dark and glossy. She was Dun, and she walked alone. Then there were two bay mares, one with a white blaze on her forehead, and one who looked much older. White Blaze, and Old Bay. Was Old Bay the lead mare, the herd mother? White Blaze had a colt following behind her. At a distance, high on the hill, a grey stallion watched over his females and his young, but Teasel ignored him. He wouldn't mind her being here.

When White Blaze and Dun went to the grass that looked nicest, Old Bay ran at them, pushed them, and sent them running away to either side. No other horse was allowed near that sweet grass until Old Bay had eaten and moved off, and Teasel knew then she had been right about her. Old Bay was in charge here.

The young colt wandered a few steps from his mother. He was learning how much freedom he could get away with, and for the fun and the joy of the bright morning, he flicked his tail and went for a run. Nobody minded as long as he stayed on his side of the brook, but when he tried to cross it Old Bay and White Blaze ran after him and nudged him back to the herd. He took the lesson easily. Fair enough. He'd have some more milk instead, and try to explore another day.

Old Bay had seen Teasel, too. She stood on her own side of the brook and tossed her head as a warning.

Teasel didn't attempt to challenge her. What would

be the point? The herd would do whatever Old Bay wanted. Instead, she turned obediently and trotted away to stand under a tree like a naughty child in a corner with her head and tail down until Old Bay returned to the herd.

For now, it was enough to know who was who. Old Bay was in charge and White Blaze and Mother were more interested in their babies than anything else. Dun was alone, and might become her friend. Sooner or later, she knew, the herd would let her join them. She grazed again, then returned to her place by the brook like a lonely little girl in a school playground. *Please let me in. Please let me play.*

When the sun was at its highest she waded across the brook, but Old Bay saw her, ran, and sent her splashing through the water again. She was tough then, that Old Bay. For two days she kept Teasel out, but on the third, Teasel waited until Old Bay was grazing far off. She set her hooves in the stream and crossed meekly with her head down, licking her lips and making chewing movements with her mouth to show them that she was small and harmless. *I'm no trouble. Honestly. I'm just a humble pony who would like to be your friend. I don't eat much.* When Mother ran at her she moved a little way off, because a new mother must not be annoyed, but she did not go back. This time, firmly and quietly, she stayed on the herd's side of the brook.

Dun made a run at her once, but Teasel had watched for a long time, and was pretty certain that she knew how to deal with her. When Dun turned and showed her heels, Teasel showed her heels, too, and laid her ears back. She advanced a few steps. She intended to become best friends with this pony, but at this stage she still had to show that she meant to stay by challenging somebody. Dun was the easiest.

For three weeks, she hovered at the edge of the herd, and every day they reminded her that she was a newcomer. She was chased away from the best grazing. The ponies bullied her, nipped her and kicked her, but she began to hold her head and tail up. She would deliberately steal a mouthful of the sweetest grass before Old Bay could chase her off. It wasn't eating the grass that mattered (oh, but it was sweet and delicious grass). What mattered to her was to say, clearly and without kicking or biting anyone, that she had as much right to live on the hill as any other pony.

The stallion watched from a distance and let them sort it out themselves. The new girl was managing well enough, and settling in. She looked like a natural hill pony. She'd stay.

Gwen sat down in the warm lounge of a nursing home.

"I'm very sorry, Mrs Tilney," she said.

Mrs Tilney had been moved from the hospital to a nursing home. She had spent the first week complaining and arguing with Matron, then decided that as she was here she may as well enjoy it. Now, she sat in her armchair by a window that opened on to a patio, watching the birds in the garden. A gardener worked his way round, weeding and snipping, with a small terrier following him about. Gwen had wondered why Mrs Tilney had asked her to bring a tennis ball. Now she understood that it was for the terrier, or rather, for Mrs Tilney to throw for him.

"Good boy!" said Mrs Tilney as the dog dropped the ball at her feet. She was enjoying his company very much. "Ready?"

Her face was still lopsided, her speech was not quite back to normal, and she still sometimes got words and phrases the wrong way round, but her hair had been washed and neatly cut. Her clothes were already covered in dog hairs, but they were new. She looked better than Gwen had ever seen her, even before the stroke.

"Jill bought new clothesh for me," she said. "I hadn't ashked her to, but she inshishted. There can't be a thing left in Spensh and Markshersh, bother it, Marksh and Spenshers." She threw the ball again, and there was a splash as it landed in a watering can.

"Oh, jolly shot good!" she exclaimed. "What do you mean, you shilly girl, what have you got to be shorry about?"

"I didn't find Teasel," said Gwen. She took the dripping wet tennis ball from the dripping wet terrier, and threw it again. "I'll keep trying, but I don't know how."

"Goodnesh me, girl, I hear you've shpent all your endweeksh flying about the . . . green thing . . . countryshide with Michael'sh mad daughter, looking for Teashel!" said Mrs Tilney. "What more could you have done?"

"I should be able to find something the size of a pony!" exclaimed Gwen. Mrs Tilney smiled a lopsided smile and curled her bony fingers over the top of her stick.

"Not if she doeshn't want to be found," she said. "You weren't the one who deshided to pack her off two countiesh away from home. Michael'sh an idiot." She took the ball from the terrier and bounced it off the fence. "I'm very fond of him. He'sh a very clever man, and a good school mashter, but he'sh sthtill an idiot. You did your besht."

"I'm afraid somebody might get hold of her and ill treat her," said Gwen.

"They'd have to catch her firsht," said Mrs Tilney, and turned the bright blue eyes on Gwen. "Remember what an outdoor girl she ish. She grew up on a Welsh hillside shomewhere. She may have a pretty little fashe, but she can look after hershelf. Anyone who arguesh with her had better out look."

A Welsh hillside, thought Gwen. She looked out towards the garden without seeing it. *Of course. Last time we saw her, she was on the Welsh borders.*

"My dear, if you think any harder, you'll have shteam coming out of your earsh," said Mrs Tilney.

"Mrs Tilney, you said she came off the hill from a wild herd," urged Gwen. "I knew that, but . . . do you know exactly where it was? Do you know where her herd lived?"

"Oh, my word!" exclaimed Mrs Tilney. "That'sh a

thought. Do you think she'sh trying to get home?"

"She might," said Gwen. "I don't know how she'd find them, but she might try. Can you remember?"

"My dear, I haven't a clue," said Mrs Tilney. "I bought her from a reshcue shenter. All thoshe hill poniesh belong to shomeone, but she changed handsh a bit before I had her."

The terrier returned, and Gwen bent her head over him to hide her disappointment.

"But all her papersh are in the houshe shomewhere," went on Mrs Tilney. "All horses have a . . . pashport. That musht have gone with her to the shtablesh new. But there are shome papersh at home."

"Oh, then can I—" began Gwen, then stopped. "I suppose Michael has the keys."

"Bother Michael!" said Mrs Tilney. "Where'sh my bandhag?"

Gwen found the old leather bag beside the chair and placed it in Mrs Tilney's lap. "Do you want me to find something?" she asked, but Mrs Tilney rummaged about with her good hand. A few old photographs and a packet of mints landed on the carpet and had to be rescued from the terrier.

"Keysh!" said Mrs Tilney firmly, as Gwen picked up a packet of tissues and a pension book from the floor. "The little one will open the . . . drawer . . . in the deshk. Teashel'sh papersh are in there. Jolly good luck to you. Now, she may not make a linebee for her old herd, and if she doesh, the chanshes are she won't find it. And if she doesh, they'll think she'sh . . . an intruder.

They'll give her the mosht almighty beating up."

Not if I can help it, thought Gwen. "I'll go straight to your house and look for the papers," she said, and was putting her jacket on when a nurse came in.

"Are you leaving now?" she asked. "That's good. Arabella gets tired easily, don't you, Arabella?"

"Don't talk shuch utter rubbish, nursh! I'm not a baby!" Mrs Tilney was saying as Gwen walked away. Gwen smiled to herself. She wasn't all that tired, then.

Gwen hated the idea of Teasel being bullied by a wild herd. She needed to act quickly. She caught the bus straight to Lady Anne Cottages, walked through the overgrown garden and unlocked the door. There was a faint smell of damp in the hall and the drab sitting room, and a cobweb hung from a lampshade.

Something wasn't right. Usually when a house had been empty, there was a heap of letters and flyers on the doormat. There was nothing here. It was too neat, and too still.

Upstairs, a floorboard creaked.

As quietly as she could Gwen stepped backwards down the hall, slipping her phone from her pocket. Once she was out of the door she could phone the police.

A door opened on the landing. Gwen kept backing away. Someone spoke.

"I know you're there," said a voice. "Get out now, and there won't be any trouble."

"Lily!" cried Gwen. "What are you doing here?"

"Oh, it's you. Hi!" called Lily, running down the stairs. "You scared the daylights out of me!" This time she was all in black apart from a pink polka-dot hairband and sandals, and yellow rubber gloves that she pulled off to hug Gwen. Then she held her at arm's length.

"Hey, what are *you* doing here?" she asked, and didn't wait for an answer. "I'm not working this week, and Dad gave me the keys to come in here and clean the house. You know what he's like. He wants Auntie Arabella to come and live with us, and that's cool. She can't stay here. She'll have to sell this house or rent it out and Dad wants it ready for people to see. As if it was up to him! They've got a plumber and a painter coming this week, so I need to be here to let them in. I offered to paint it myself, but they wouldn't let me. So tell! Why are you here?"

"I need Teasel's records," said Gwen. "If they show where she comes from we can guess at where she's going. Mrs Tilney says to look in her desk."

The elegant little writing desk stood in a corner of the bedroom. The lock was stiff and the key difficult to turn, but when the drawer finally opened, papers spilled out over their hands. Some were so grubby and yellow with age that Gwen handled them delicately with her fingertips, while Lily left her to it and went to try on Mrs Tilney's hats in the mirror. There were faded newspaper cuttings of births, marriages and deaths, and photos of a young, pretty Mrs Tilney with her husband. There were letters that Gwen pushed quickly to one side because she felt they were too private even to handle, and a fat brown envelope stuffed with papers.

"This is it!" she exclaimed. Lily took off a straw boater and came to look.

"Look, it's got Teasel's name on it," said Gwen, "and her mark! Look at the arrow, and the number underneath it – that's Teasel's freeze brand!"

"What's a freeze brand?" asked Lily.

"It's the mark on her back," said Gwen. "Horses have a freeze brand so you can identify them. Sometimes they have microchips. But look, on the back of the envelope, that's Teasel's mark!"

She leafed through the sheaf of papers, which looked as if they'd been dropped in a stableyard and trodden on a few times. There were records from the vet and from the rescue centre, and finally, out drifted a flimsy receipt so faded that she could hardly read it.

"It says something like ... Travon ... then Carr – Carradon?" She held it up to the light. "Can you make it out?"

Lily peered at it. "Travon-in-Carneddau!" she said. "I've heard of that. Well, I've heard of Carnie-thing. It's in some Welsh mountains somewhere."

"Do you know whereabouts?" asked Gwen.

"Sort of," said Lily. "I've been to Travon village before. We can get there – it's only about an hour and a half's drive from Mum and Dad! You up for it? It's school holidays, right?"

"But you're supposed to be here getting the house ready!" said Gwen.

The brightness lost Lily's face for a moment. "Yeah,"

she said. "And Mum and Dad are both teaching summer schools, so they can't come, and we can't go to Travie Carnie thing without somebody being here. Let's think of someone."

"There's Mum, depending on what the twins are doing," said Gwen, and then added awkwardly, "or, if we're stuck, there's always Charlotte."

It wasn't easy to suggest Charlotte. She wasn't part of the Teasel-and-Lily world, and Gwen didn't particularly want her to be. But they had to find Teasel.

"OK, that's cool," decided Lily. "Pack a bag." Within an hour, they were back in the car.

Chapter Ten

They stayed that night with Michael and Jill. The next day was sunny, with a breeze. At last, after a long drive, they found Travon-in-Carneddau, but the more they explored the Welsh hill country the less the map made any sense. Time and again they stopped to ask for directions, and still got lost. Eventually a road sign indicating wild ponies helped, and a little further on they came to a forest car park where Gwen got out and read the notices pinned up on the notice board.

WARNING

Wild ponies roam freely in the forest.
You are advised to stay on the footpaths.
Do not attempt to feed the ponies.
Wild ponies may bite, bolt, or kick.

She went back to the car and took her helmet from the boot. "Just in case," she said.

"In case what?" asked Lily.

"In case anything bites, bolts or kicks me," said Gwen simply. She lifted out a head collar and a lead rope, too, but she felt she'd rather not slip the collar over Teasel's head. She wanted Teasel to follow her freely.

The day was beautiful, a perfect riding day, and Gwen would have enjoyed it much more if she hadn't been anxious about what was happening to Teasel. Butterflies settled on one flower and another, bees made a fuss in the heather, and birds sang above them. Little streams ran through the forest floor, the water so clear that the pebbles underneath glowed like an enchanted city. As they climbed higher there were fewer trees and the view became clearer. Somewhere, something whinnied.

"Listen!" said Gwen. "Whereabouts did that come from?"

"From the right, I think," said Lily, and they listened again. "Definitely right."

A narrow, rocky path led them struggling uphill, over a rise, and down again. At last, out of breath and a bit scratched, they came to a clearing so well hidden that as Gwen said afterwards, they wouldn't have found it if they hadn't heard the whinny. A brook formed a natural barrier on one side.

A young mare stood cropping the grass under a silver birch tree, with her dappled foal lying beside her.

Not far off, a dark pony stood quietly, and a bay mare lifted her head to look at them. She watched them for a while, then walked away to drink from the brook. Then from under the shade of the trees, tossing her head, Teasel trotted into view.

Gwen gave a gasp that was almost a cry. She pressed her hands against her mouth to force herself to be quiet.

"That's her!" she whispered. "The little golden pony!"

"Oh, isn't she gorgeous!" breathed Lily.

Teasel had mud on her pale golden coat, grass and dirt were tangled in her tail, and she needed a good brushing, but she was as lovely as ever. She gathered speed, cantered up to the old mare, and shouldered her out of the way. Gwen gasped again.

"There you are!" said Lily. "They haven't beaten her up!"

"Maybe they have," said Gwen quietly, "and she fought back. I don't think they'd let her in easily. She's coped with it. But she shouldn't have pushed the bay mare."

"What did she do it for?" asked Lily.

"I think it was a challenge," answered Gwen. "She wants to be in charge of this herd."

"Hey, good for her!" said Lily, and quietly retreated a little way. "If you don't need me just now, I'll wander off and sketch a bit. I won't be far away; call if you need me."

Gwen was left alone with the horses. The old bay mare pushed back against Teasel, and Teasel turned away with a flick of her tail.

So this was it. The quest to find Teasel, wet weekend after wet weekend, was over. Gwen took a breath to call her name, and did not.

Not yet. She waited. Teasel walked away carelessly, like a child dawdling on her way home from school. Now and again she lowered her head to graze or drink. Gwen sat down on a rock and watched.

Teasel wandered further away, munched grass, stamped a hoof and snorted down her nose. Everything about her was so familiar that seeing her again was like coming home. Gwen longed to call her, pat her, and let Teasel nuzzle her and hunt for mints in her pocket. She ached for the feel of Teasel's warm face against her own. But she went on observing, quietly.

Teasel approached the dark pony and stood head to head with her. *That's her friend*, thought Gwen, seeing the way they teamed up together. *A new friend, like Hattie.* She glanced round to see Lily at a distance, sketching, absorbed in what she was doing. No hurry, then. Here in Carneddau the sun was shining, the breeze was soft, and the ponies were enjoying the grass. A perfect day.

She thought of Mrs Tilney's house, the paddock, the bridle path. She remembered Teasel's terror at going into the horsebox. Teasel stood still with her friend, and didn't challenge the older horse again.

But she will, thought Gwen. *She'll wait for the right time.* She didn't know what the other horses had done to bully Teasel. But Teasel had survived. She had fought her way to her place in the herd, and been accepted, but that wasn't enough. She was aiming to be queen of the hill, and she'd probably succeed one day. She was outside, and happy.

Was this "home"? Was that how Teasel saw it now?

Moving slowly and smoothly, not wanting to alarm the herd, Gwen stood up and took a few steps forward. She had come here to bring Teasel back. For Teasel's sake and Mrs Tilney's she had to try. But now, seeing Teasel amongst the herd, she knew that it wasn't up to her, not any more. Teasel had to choose. She had thought that Teasel would choose her, but now she remembered what Mrs Tilney always said – *she's an outdoor girl*.

She clicked her tongue. "Teasel!" she called.

At the sound of her name, Teasel raised her head and looked directly at Gwen. That look, the wide, elegant face and the deep dark eyes watching her from under the fringe, made Gwen want to run to her and hug her like a best friend. But that was the last thing she should do.

"Teasel," she said again. "Darling girl!"

Teasel looked back at her and twitched her ears. Gwen saw the understanding, the recognition in the large brown eyes. Teasel remembered her.

You know me, don't you, Teasel. You know I gave you food. I looked after you and groomed you. Remember that; remember we're friends. Don't remember the last thing I did – Gwen could hardly bear to think of it now; she hated herself for it – *don't remember me leading you into the trailer. Is that what you're thinking of? Is that why you're laying back your ears and standing apart from me? Don't! Please, don't stay away from me!*

"Mrs Tilney's been asking about you," said Gwen. Her hand closed on the packet of mints from her pocket, and stayed closed. If she offered a mint, Teasel would probably take it and Gwen could slip on the head collar, lead her away – and then what? Sooner or later, whatever they did, Teasel would have to go into a horsebox again.

She wouldn't entice Teasel away with a mint. It would be a cheap trick, bribing her with a sweet. *Anyway, it would be stupid to offer her food. They'd all want some, and I'd get trampled in the rush.*

She stayed where she was, gazing at Teasel, filling all her heart and soul with her beautiful golden pony, her friend. She called once more.

"Teasel!"

Teasel took one step, then another. A shiver of hope ran through Gwen, then Teasel lowered her head and grazed again, ignoring her.

Gwen squeezed her eyes shut. The disappointment was so crushing, it could not be happening. But when she looked again, Teasel still stood with her head down.

She had called Teasel's name three times. In those stories that she loved so much when she was little, things always happened in threes. Three sisters, three tasks, three wishes. If Teasel didn't come now, she wouldn't come at all.

"If you want to, you can follow me," she said. "But if you want to stay here, I understand. Mrs Tilney will understand, too. We just want you to be happy, and safe. Have a lovely life, darling girl."

She turned and walked away, still listening for any sound behind her, hoping, still hoping and longing, for the soft tread of hooves and Teasel's warm breath on her neck. There were a few sounds of hooves on heather, then nothing. She folded her lips tightly and went on walking. When she couldn't bear it any longer she rubbed her eyes, and turned.

Teasel had gone.

Somehow, though Gwen could hardly see her way through her tears, she stumbled down the hill towards the car park. Fast footsteps behind her made her turn. Lily was flying down the hill, her satchel flapping at her side.

"Gwen, what happened!" she cried, and reached out to her.

It was a long time before Gwen could say anything. When at last she had finished sobbing in Lily's arms, she told her everything.

"She's happy," she said. "She's found her family."

It was too soon to go home to the family clutter and the constant voices. She needed to spend one more night in the quiet of Michael and Jill's house, with Lily, who had been through all this with her, and understood what to ask and what not to ask. But in her head was the picture of Jack perched on top of Teasel as she led them round the paddock. Tomorrow she would do what Teasel had done. She would go back to her family.

"Love found a way," she said to Lily that evening. "I just wish it wasn't this one."

"It's because you loved her that you let her go," said Lily.

Teasel grazed alone, ignoring Dun. She was puzzled and uneasy.

There were two worlds. One was this spacious hill with the other ponies who thought and ate and lived as she did. They understood each other, and observed the rules of the herd. If they needed shelter they stood under trees, they drank from the stream, and their food was the good sweet grass under their hooves. Occasionally people came up here, but it was the ponies' world, not the world of the people.

But she had lived in that world, too, and she remembered all too well that there had been a box in that world, a hard, noisy thing that shut her in and carried her away from her home. She had hated that box. She knew, though, that there had been good things too, kind hands to clean and brush her, and sweet, exciting tastes to eat. More than anything there had been her old Arabella and Gwen.

My Gwen. We were happy together.

But now Gwen had appeared on the hill, even though she shouldn't be there. She didn't belong in this world. It was a puzzle that did not fit. Why was the girl here?

Chapter Eleven

Back in the world of her own home and family, Gwen went to the nursing home to visit Mrs Tilney. She waited by the open garden doors in the lounge holding a little gift-wrapped box of chocolates and watching the terrier gnawing contentedly at the remains of the tennis ball. When she heard a steady tap-shuffle from the hall, she turned to meet Mrs Tilney. One eyelid still drooped – perhaps it always would – but the bright mischievous light was in her eyes. She smiled when she saw Gwen. On one side she leaned on a nurse, and the other hand trembled on her stick.

"Slow and steady, Arabella," advised the nurse loudly.

"I know dear, shlow and shteady as the tortoishe shaid," said Mrs Tilney. "I think it wash the tortoishe?

Or wash it the shnail? Snail. With an s. You know, the shnail – snail, going to Jerushalem."

Gwen smiled. She hadn't a clue what Mrs Tilney was talking about, but her voice was already stronger and clearer than before.

"You're doing really well, Arabella," said the nurse, lowering her carefully into a chair.

"Thank you, my dear. I'm going for a gallop round the jumpsh thish afternoon," she said. She kissed Gwen, told her off for buying her chocolates, and asked,

"How did you get on? Any shign of the old girl?"

Gwen told her the story. Mrs Tilney listened with both hands folded over her stick.

"So," finished Gwen at last, "I'm sorry. I know I should have brought her back, because she's yours, after all, but she'd made herself at home with the herd. If you do want her back, I suppose we could see about getting her rounded up." She knew she had to offer this, but it felt wrong. It would be a betrayal, to send people to the hill to bring Teasel down. She'd already betrayed her once by leading her into that trailer.

"Oh, my dear," said Mrs Tilney. "It'sh ecshactly what I would have done. If she'sh happy on the hill, she may ash well stay there. But you'll mish her."

"I'll go up and check on her sometimes for you," promised Gwen. She'd have to find a way of getting there without relying on Lily for transport, but she'd think of something. "If she'd followed me, it would have been different, but she chose."

It still hurt to know that Teasel had chosen the hill, and not her. She could understand it, but there was an empty place in her life now, and a long summer without Teasel stretched before her.

"How long are you staying here?" she asked.

"I gather they're letting me out of prishon – prison – necsht week, if I behave myshelf," she said. "If I don't, they might kick me out early. Then I'm renting out the cottage and going to live with Michael and Jill. They're filling their house with sh . . . safety railsh and whatnot. They've even got one of thoshe chairsh s . . . so I can shlide down the banishter in style. And I'm getting one of thoshe zhimmer walking things. Don't supposhe I'll use it, ecshept for whacking Michael." She smiled the crooked smile. "But I'm afraid Michael'sh right. I can't go on living on my own. I can't look after myshelf, never mind Teashel."

For the first time, her voice became unsteady and her eyes filled. She turned her head away, blinked, blew her nose noisily and with determination, and said, "Well, there you are. I will be tempted to wind Michael up, but I shall try to resisht."

"I'll miss you," said Gwen.

"No you jolly well won't, my girl, you'll come and see me!" ordered Mrs Tilney. "Get your father to shove you on a train at thish end, and Jill can shcoop you up at the other. And I hear that you and Lara . . . Lilac . . . what's her name? . . . Lily, get on like a house on fire. She's awfully good fun, ishn't she? Mad as a hatter, you know, but shuch a jolly girl! I think I can quite enjoy moving in with them, now that I've . . . what'sh the exshpression . . . round my head?"

"Now you've got your head around it?" suggested Gwen.

"Yes. That. I'll enjoy having the family around. Eshpecially when it includes you and . . . don't tell me! I know it. Tall white thing. Flower. Lily."

Gwen was about to go, when she had an idea.

"Have you got anything I can draw on?" she asked. A hunt through Mrs Tilney's handbag produced a little notebook and a pencil.

"This will help you to remember her name," she said. Her sketch of a lily wasn't anything like as good as Lily's artwork, but it was recognizable, and just to make it clear she wrote "Lily" underneath.

At home, she took out her newest treasure. While she had been watching Teasel, Lily had been sitting on the hill, steadily sketching. From those sketches she had completed three pictures of Teasel, and given them to Gwen to take home. Gwen's favourite was the one of Teasel trotting with her head up, the turf around her hooves. Lily had captured her look, the way she moved, and the streaks of mud on her golden coat. Looking at it made Gwen happy and hurt at the same time.

When she could she'd get it framed, but in the meantime she posted it up in her room. She had meant at first to put it over her bed, then changed her mind and hung it on a wall where she'd see it as soon as she woke up in the mornings. Teasel, always to be treasured.

Gwen found that she could live without Teasel, if only because she had to. When the school holidays were over she enjoyed seeing her friends at school again, and there were a few riding lessons, too. Mrs Tilney, as planned, moved in with Michael and Jill.

Gwen no longer felt so out of place at school. Life with Teasel had given her confidence. Sometimes at weekends she was able to meet Lily, and they'd drive up to Carneddau and watch for Teasel. Each time, Gwen sat at a distance, observing the herd, while Lily sketched horses, or acorns, or fallen leaves. As autumn went on Gwen looked forward to Christmas as she always did, but this year New Year would be special, too. She would be spending it at the Baileys' house with Lily and Mrs Tilney. She was counting the hours as well as the days.

On New Year's Eve, Lily and Gwen were to drive to Carneddau to see Teasel. The evening before, they sat in Mrs Tilney's sitting room drinking hot chocolate and playing tiddlywinks. The rule was that everybody had to play with their weaker hand so that Mrs Tilney wouldn't be at a disadvantage. In the background, the television talked to itself. Mrs Tilney flipped a tiddlywink that would have hit Gwen if she hadn't ducked, then looked past her at the television.

"I say, Gwen, turn up the blah-blah box, will you?" she said.

"Heavy snowfalls are expected in North Wales and the Welsh Borders tomorrow," said the announcer. "The AA is advising motorists not to travel over New Year unless absolutely necessary."

"I hope we can still get up to Carneddau," said Gwen.

"It's cool, we'll be fine," said Lily. "They always say that. Your turn, Auntie Arabella."

A tiddlywink shot into the air and landed in Lily's mug of chocolate. "I say, hole in one!" cried Mrs Tilney. "One of her rugs is here somewhere, goodness knows why. You will take it, won't you, when you go to see her?"

"Then we'll have to get there," said Gwen. "She needs her rug."

"Cool," said Lily. "A bit of snow won't stop us, sweetie."

The next day Gal was loaded with Teasel's rug and – just in case they were stranded in snow – wellies, flasks, sandwiches, a torch and a shovel. Gwen and Lily were on the way to Carneddau when the flakes began to fall. At first they came lightly, tumbling prettily round the car as if Lily had driven into a Christmas storybook, but by the time they reached Travon village they could barely see the road ahead. Keeping their heads down, they dashed to the nearest cafe for toasties and hot drinks before they set out for the drive into the hills. A fire burned in the grate, a Christmas tree sparkled in a corner and lights twinkled from the ceiling. Gwen curled her hands round the hot mug of chocolate as she watched the snow falling. She couldn't even see the other side of the street.

"Hi?" said Lily. "Are you in?"

"I was just wondering how we're going to get up there," she said, and turned to the waitress. "Do you know how the ponies on the hill are coping with the snow?" she asked.

"I suppose they're fine," said the waitress cheerfully. "They live out there, rain or shine, all year round. They're used to it. They're tough. The owners keep an eye on them. Some of the men who own them were up yesterday with hay – my brother went up with them. He works with horses, so he looks out for the hill ponies too. There are lots of people with horses by here, and they all keep an eye open for the herd. If there are any worries the RSPCA go and check on them."

And they're not going to find Teasel neglected, thought Gwen. That wasn't going to happen. The owners were responsible for the horses, and she was the nearest thing Teasel had to an owner just now.

"Were you planning on going up today?" asked the waitress. "You won't get the car up, but there's a footpath. It's a long walk at the best of times, but it's the best way to do it in this weather. Mind, you'll have to move if you're going to get up there and back before dark. I've got a walker's map – you'll need one."

They took the map and Lily's torch from the car, and took turns to carry Teasel's heavy rug. As usual, Gwen carried a head collar and lead rope because, as she said to Lily, it was always a good idea to take those when you were around horses. They struggled uphill through slush, mud and ice, but that didn't stop Lily pausing to photograph the trees. "Look at those shapes!" she exclaimed. "The sky through the branches, and the snow, and the grey-white look in the sky!"

Gwen curled her toes against the cold and huddled her shoulders up. "It's beautiful," she agreed. "But it'll be dark by four. Can I have another look at the map?"

But the way ahead didn't seem clear and they were constantly brushing snow off the map as they walked on up the hill. With white trees in the white landscape, it wasn't easy to work out which path was which. With every step the snow fell harder, the path grew steeper, and Gwen's fingers and toes stung with cold. *Soon I will be numb*, she thought, *and then I won't feel it any more.* Patches of ice made them slither and grab at each other, and at trees and branches. When at last they reached a clearing, gasping for breath, they turned to look down.

"Oh, wow!" they both said.

For the first time, Gwen realized how far up they were. Snow-laden trees in the light of the setting sun shone like gold, almost too bright to see. Below them, lights were coming on in the village. Windows glowed, warm and inviting. Strings of lights twinkled on the trees and shone from Christmas trees between open curtains.

It was so close, and a world away. And the sun that made the snow so fiery gold would disappear in half an hour. Dark was coming.

"Hold that a minute," said Lily, and bundled the rug into Gwen's arms. "My sock's gone down inside my boot. Hang on while I get it straight."

She steadied herself against a tree trunk. Gwen was struggling to fold the rug and hold the torch so that Lily could see what she was doing when Lily shrieked. Then she wasn't there.

Teasel was now alone.

In the last two weeks she had won her challenges against Old Bay. She had grown confident. When she lived with people she had been well fed and cared for, but she knew that the air of the wild high hills was doing her good. She felt strong. After the herd had accepted her, and Dun had become her friend, she had been able to challenge Old Bay. She would eat where the grazing was best and choose where she rested. If other ponies nipped her or stamped at her, she could do that, too. She could turn her back on ponies she wanted to ignore, and they came to see that Teasel had authority. Little by little, she had become the lead mare, the queen of the herd.

Since then, the foul fierce weather had upset her. She hadn't remembered how bitterly cold these hills could be. Her confidence was shaken, and Old Bay had seen it.

In the morning, before the worst of the weather had begun, men had arrived with bales of hay, and Teasel, as the leader, had gone to eat first. But Old Bay had seen her chance, kicked her hard, and chased her away.

So now Teasel stood away from the others, on the edge of the clearing, punished and waiting to be let in again. Not even her friend Dun dared stand near her to keep her warm.

The kick had cut her leg, and the icy cold made the wound sting. She remembered being hurt before and the Gwen girl had healed her. But there was no girl now.

"Gwen!" called Lily from somewhere.

Gwen turned sharply. She still couldn't see Lily.

"Where are you?" she called. "Lily? Where are you?"

She heard Lily laugh, but it wasn't her usual laugh. It sounded as if it took an effort. She shone the torch high and low until she saw Lily pulling herself up from the ground. Gwen reached out a hand.

"No. I'm OK," said Lily. "Don't, I don't want to pull you over. I'll get myself up." She grabbed at the tree trunk, pulling herself up hand over hand. "I was trying to get my boot right and the ground was slippery. There's a slope here, and my foot slipped under me. Just give me a second or two, I'm OK."

But she wasn't. Her face in the torch beam was white, and her mouth was tight with pain.

"Have you twisted your foot?" asked Gwen. "Don't put your weight on it! Stay still!" But Lily didn't hear, or didn't want to. She went on pulling herself up on the tree trunk, then stood, holding on first with both hands, then with one.

Gwen put down the rug and reached out a hand to

her. After a moment's pause, Lily rubbed one grubby hand on her jacket and held it out. Gwen took it. Lily held on tightly. Cautiously, she let go of the tree, put her foot down, tried to put her weight on it, and fell with a sharp cry of pain. Gwen tried to hold her, and fell too. On her hands and knees in frozen mud and darkness, Gwen held on to Lily's hand and heard her wince softly.

"Sorry, Gwen," gasped Lily, who could hardly speak.

"Don't say that!" said Gwen. "Here, let me have a look."

Alone in her corner of disgrace, Teasel heard a voice she trusted. Then somebody said "Gwen". Teasel's memory stirred. She felt echoes of something good, as good as the sweep and brush of grooming, as good as sweet apples and moorland and a warm rug over her back, and something more, a warmth and a feeling of goodness and care that went with the name and the touch and voice – "Gwen". The way in to all these things was "Gwen". That was the word. *Gwen*. She tramped steadily through the snow.

"Help me get my boot off," said Lily.

"I think you're supposed to leave your boot on, to keep the swelling down," advised Gwen, but Lily had pulled the boot from her right foot. It was already swollen.

RICE, Gwen remembered from some long-ago first-aid training when she was in the Guides. Rest, Ice, Compression and Elevation. Of course Lily's foot would be resting, there was no way she could step on it. There was plenty of ice, or at least snow, and she could bind it up tightly with something. Lily was wearing two pairs of socks. One wet sock would be enough.

"Hold still," she said, and pulled off her gloves. Her fingers were clumsy with cold, but with Lily holding the torch she managed to bind up the foot and ankle tightly. She tied the sock in a knot and gently pulled the other one over it.

"That'll do for now," she said, but she needed help. "If you wrap Teasel's rug round yourself, and I go down to—"

From somewhere behind her, a horse blew down its nose. Hooves crunched the snow. Gwen looked round, shining the torch, and the cry came from deep in her heart.

"Teasel!"

Yes. It was Teasel.

It was months since she had stood so close to Teasel, and then Teasel had chosen the herd. But now she stood patiently, watching, her ears forward.

Gwen scrambled to her feet, wiped her hands on her jacket, and aimed the torch a little to one side of Teasel, not wanting to shine it in her eyes and scare her. The beam of light picked up the wide, dark stain of blood on her leg.

"Darling girl, what's happened to you?" she called, and scrambled up the hill to her. Lily tried to follow, but then there was a little squeak of pain.

"Lily, don't move!" she said. Lily pressed her hand to her mouth. "Are you OK?"

There was a pause, then Lily nodded.

"Cool," she said. "I thought I was going to throw up, but I'm fine."

Gwen took a deep breath and prepared to sort this out. *If you want a thing doing, do it yourself.* Lily was hurt, hurting so much that she was nearly sick. She may be in shock, and hypothermia could set in if she wasn't somewhere warm soon. Teasel had recognized her, but Teasel was hurt, too. *I really wish I had some help here.*

She tried her phone, but there was no signal on the snowbound hilltop. She tucked the rug more tightly round Lily. Lily muttered a low "thank you", but she seemed too cold even to speak. Gwen plodded through mud back to Teasel.

"Now, Teasel," she said. "Let's look at you."

Teasel's ears twitched forward. She stepped towards the known, loved voice. Then Gwen was standing in her old place, her true place, with her arm round Teasel's neck and her face pressed against her.

"Sweetheart, Teasel, my Teasel, it's me. It's your Gwen. I've got you."

She wanted to stay for ever in the torchlit snow, holding Teasel's unresisting warmth against her. But Teasel and Lily were hurt.

"Now, darling girl," she said, "let's have a look at that leg. Stand. That's it."

She knelt, glancing up towards the other ponies in case any of them should resent her and charge at them, but they stood huddled together, ignoring the outcast and the stranger. With the torch under her arm Gwen examined Teasel's leg, dipping her scarf in snow and dabbing it at the wound. Teasel stood still, knowing that this had happened before. It was good.

"Oh, it's only a graze!" she said. "A teeny one! Let me see you walk. Teasel, walk on."

One . . . two . . . three . . . four, and again . . . one . . . two . . . three . . . four. That was a good, steady sound. There was no limp, nothing uneven.

"I think you're all right, sweetheart," she said. She hugged the familiar softness of Teasel's neck and mane, wet and roughened by winter on the hill, and offered an apple from the palm of her hand. "Now, darling girl, I need you to help me."

Chapter Twelve

Michael Bailey remarked to Jill that Lily hadn't called.

"I'll leave a message on her phone," said Jill. "She should be all right – she's very sensible."

At Gwen's home, Mum was telling Dad what a pity it was, Gwen not being home for New Year. "But she likes being at the Baileys'," she remarked. "I expect she'll phone later."

The girl at the cafe noticed that the little car was still parked, with at least four inches of snow on the roof. Those two girls had gone away up the hill to the ponies. Had anyone seen them come down again? She took out her phone.

"Hi, it's Carys," she said. "Have you been up to feed

the ponies today? Only there's two girls gone up there, and it's dark now, and I haven't seen them come back. Their car's still parked outside the cafe. I just thought you might have seen them."

Gwen needed to do her thinking aloud. She talked to Teasel.

"I can't leave Lily alone," she said, "so I need you, darling girl. I'm not going down the way we came up, it's too hard. We're going across the clearing to the road, because I know where I am with that road. It's the long way round but we won't hurry. And we can keep each other warm. Good girl. It's time you had a mint."

Side by side, Teasel and Gwen walked back to the edge of the clearing. "Stand," ordered Gwen, and Teasel stood obediently. Gwen slithered over to Lily and found her shivering under the rug. She smiled bravely, but with torchlight on her face she looked so white that Gwen was terrified.

"You're going to be fine," Gwen reassured her, but she hoped she sounded more confident than she felt. "We're going back to those warm windows in the village. Hold on to me."

It was only a few yards to the place where Teasel waited, but Lily was on her hands and knees for half of it. Gwen slipped on Teasel's head collar and clipped the lead rope to it.

"Now," she said, "we have to get you on to the pony. Put your good foot – Teasel, stand still – put your good foot into my hands."

It took a lot of heaving and a few winces and mutterings from Lily, but at last she was on Teasel's back. She grimaced, then smiled faintly.

"It's like sitting on a roof!" she gasped.

"Horses have bony backs," Gwen told her. "Now sit up as straight as you can and keep your heels down." She shone the torch across the clearing. "Teasel, walk on."

That's the hardest bit done. Lily's up, and staying up. All I have to do now is get us all back.

"Good girl, Teasel," she said as she led her away from the herd. "I'm sorry I'm doing this to you. I know you're cold; I know you haven't carried anyone for a long time. Do you remember the moors in spring? And the day you bucked me off?"

Talking to Teasel was important. It reassured her, and it did the same for Gwen, too. It also took her mind from the cold, the wet clothes, and the deep, hostile darkness outside the circle of torchlight. Now and again she stopped to check the phone, but there was still no signal.

A little further on the torchlight showed her a broken signpost by a stile, and her heart felt heavy. She recognized that signpost, and knew how far they still had to go to the main road. She patted Teasel's neck.

"Keep going, darling girl. You're a star," she said. After the next bend in the road, she tried the phone again.

"Yes!" she told Lily. "It's working!"

The freezing air made her hands shake so badly that

she could hardly use the phone. At last, there was a voice at the other end.

"Ambulance, please," said Gwen. "My friend's injured and she can't walk. And we're in a snowstorm. Sorry, you're breaking up? We're at Carneddau – that's Carneddau, near Travon . . . no, Travon-in-Carneddau, trying to get down to the village. No, there isn't a postcode, we're in the hills – Lily, do you know the road number? Sorry, I can't hear you?"

The signal failed, and failed again when Gwen kept trying. There was nothing to do but to go on, slowly. At last, when they rounded a bend, she gave a cry of joy.

"Lily! Look at that!"

They were looking down on street lights and Christmas lights. The road was far away, but at last they could see it.

"Beautiful!" said Lily. She leaned forward to pat Teasel's neck, but she swayed and Gwen caught her.

"Hang on!" she said. "Lily, can you still sit up?"

"I'm fine," Lily insisted. With a bit of a push from Gwen, she straightened up.

"We're nearly there now," said Gwen. They weren't, but it might make them feel better. She kept her eyes on the lights.

"Keep going, Teasel," she said. "You should get a medal for this. And the best hay in the country. Here's a mint to be going on with. Good girl."

She measured out the road in mints after that – one at the gate marked "Private", one at the fallen tree, one at the telegraph pole – but her hands were so numb that she dropped that one, and Lily nearly fell off when Teasel put her head down to find it. She'd have to keep one back for the moment when it would all be over, when Lily could be handed over to paramedics. Then they'd find a place for Teasel, and for herself, too.

"Would you stay in a stable, girl, if I was in there with you?" she said. "We could fall asleep in the straw together and keep each other warm."

Nearly there. *Good girl, Teasel, my star, my darling girl.* Then at last, to Gwen's great joy, lifting her heart, a light was coming towards them and a voice was calling out, "Is that you? You that went to see the ponies?"

A girl carrying a torch was trudging uphill to meet them, almost submerged in an enormous padded anorak and a woolly hat. She lowered the torch as she drew nearer.

"I was worried about you!" she said. "I'm Carys from the cafe. I thought you'd been gone a long time." She turned to call out to somebody else. "I've found them. They've got a pony with them, so don't go shouting out and scaring it."

Gwen forgot the cold. They were back; they were safe. She led Teasel on to the road, turning off the torch that she wouldn't need again tonight. Instead of the treacherous path there was pavement under the snow, and street lights shone round them. Carys from the cafe was hugging warmth into her, someone was lifting Lily down and taking care of her, pulling off her gloves and rubbing her hands. They tried to do the same for Gwen, but she turned, wrapped both arms round Teasel's neck, and stood still, holding her.

"That's it, my darling girl," she said. "Well done. That's it."

There was one mint left. She gave it to Teasel, and turned to the girl from the cafe.

"Is there anywhere I can take my pony?" she asked. "She needs looking after."

"*Your* pony?" asked the girl. "But I thought she was one of—"

"She's Gwen's pony," put in Lily, her voice still low with pain and cold.

"Well, you could—" began the girl, but nobody heard what she said next. With screaming sirens and flashing blue lights the ambulance swung round the corner. From Teasel came a terrible, crying whinny as she reared up, swerved, and lurched towards the road. Swinging off balance, Gwen hung on with both hands to the rope, fighting to turn Teasel's head away from the flashing lights, though it seemed that all she could do was to stay on her feet and hang on, hang on. . . If Teasel bolted, she would be lost again, she would be in the road. . . Somebody had come to the other side and was holding the head collar, but still Teasel fought, throwing her head up and showing the whites of her eyes. The siren stopped, but Teasel still struggled to escape.

"Get back! Everyone!" yelled Gwen, but most of the people around them were already scattering, staying clear of the wild hooves. She clicked her tongue and softened her voice, putting one hand on Teasel's neck.

"Teasel, stand, girl, stand! Good girl! Stand! Shh. It's all right. Shh, now. Good girl. Come on, now."

Walking might distract Teasel from her fear. Gwen clicked her tongue again.

"Teasel," she said, "walk on." Firmly she turned Teasel away from the scene and began to walk.

She had hardly expected it to work – she knew how terrified Teasel was of loud noises – but the wild struggling and head tossing had stopped. The gleam of fear left Teasel's eyes as she walked by Gwen's side. Her ears were still flattened back, but she walked, staying close to the one person here she knew.

So it's still there, thought Gwen as she walked steadily, calmly, at Teasel's side. Gwen wanted to cry with relief. Teasel and Gwen, just as they had first walked round the paddock together. They had worked their way down the icy hill in the darkness and Teasel trusted her again, and did as she asked.

"Teasel, stand," she ordered, and looked over her shoulder. The ambulance doors were open now, and paramedics were kneeling beside Lily, looking into her white face and asking her questions. There was nothing there to alarm Teasel, but all the same, it might be better to keep her away from the scene a little longer.

"Well done, darling girl," she said. "You brave girl."

Stroking Teasel's neck, looking at the long fringe, Gwen thought that it was the rule of three again. All those months ago, when Teasel had heard the fire alarm, she had bolted. She had run away from the stables at Kennedy Barns, too. But this time, terrified as she was, she had stayed. *I was with her, and she stayed.*

"Well done," she said again, wishing she still had a mint to reward her. "You stay here with me."

The man who had held the head collar was walking to meet them, carrying a torch that he shone on the ground so that it didn't dazzle her or alarm Teasel.

"Calmed down, has she?" he asked gently.

"She's getting there," said Gwen, glad to have someone to talk to. "How's Lily?"

"They're getting her fixed up now," he said. "Shall I hold your horse while you go and see? Now that you've walked her, she'll probably be all right. Take the torch if you want it."

Gwen looked at Teasel's ears. They were pricked up and she stood still, with no stamping or tail swishing.

"Teasel, stand," said Gwen. She could see that the man was calm and confident around horses, and that would help Teasel to be calm, too, so she left them and walked back to the ambulance. Lily was sitting inside, talking to Jill on her phone while a young woman paramedic examined her foot. It was bruised and looked horribly swollen.

"Look, it's purple!" said Lily, smiling bravely past the paramedic. "I love purple!"

"And it may be fractured," said the paramedic. "We'll take you to hospital and get that X-rayed." She looked at Gwen. "You're her friend – do you want to come with her?"

She still needed to find somewhere for Teasel.

Come to that, she didn't know where she and Lily would spend the night, now that Lily couldn't drive them home.

"We can look after your pony, if you want to go with her," said Carys. She picked up the rug that Gwen had dropped when she was struggling to hold Teasel. "The man that's with her now, that's my brother Gareth. He knows loads of people with stableyards – he'll find somewhere."

Teasel was standing contentedly with Gareth. Gwen frowned. Lily. Teasel. Who needed her the most?

"I'm fine," said Lily. "And I've got Mum at the end of the phone, so don't worry about me."

"I'd rather stay with Teasel," said Gwen. "We've only just found each other again – it's a long story. She's hurt her leg, and she's in a strange place."

"Teasel!" said Carys. "I was wondering where I've heard that before! The one there was all the fuss about? Tearaway Teasel?"

Gwen smiled. "Not any more," she said. "At least, I hope not."

Lily was still talking happily to Jill and telling her what had happened when the ambulance doors closed. Gareth and Carys, who seemed to know everyone in the village and a lot about horses, made some phone calls, then walked with Gwen to a large, rambling house with a garden, and some sort of paddock behind it.

"There are stables here, but they've all got horses in them just now," said Gareth. "But there's a shelter."

"She'd much prefer that," said Gwen.

The shelter was like the one in Teasel's own paddock at Mrs Tilney's house. Gwen led her to it and fastened the lead rope to a ring in the wall. Gareth brought straw for Teasel to rest on, hay and a bucket of water.

"You've been so kind," said Gwen. "Thanks ever so much. Please. . ." she didn't like to ask for anything else, but she knew Teasel so well, ". . .are there any grooming brushes here?"

"You're keen!" said Gareth with a grin. "There's a tack room at the end of the block, I'll get some from there."

"Now, darling girl," said Gwen when she had the box of brushes in her hands. She had forgotten about being chilled, damp and tired. She examined Teasel's feet as she always did, and ran her hand down each leg in turn to check for swellings or injuries. She cleaned the graze again. Then, for the first time since Teasel had been taken away, Gwen steadily brushed the mud out of her coat and the softness into it while Teasel snorted and nuzzled at her jacket. Gwen could feel the pony's tense muscles relax under her hand.

Teasel was so relaxed that when the grooming was finished and her rug was on she gave a snort and a sigh and lay down in the straw, folding her forelegs elegantly beneath her. Gwen knelt beside her.

"I wish I had a camera," she said, stroking her. Teasel's coat was deep and soft, and Gwen curled up beside her, resting her head on the warm golden body. "You're beautiful. And you're lovely and warm. You rest now. I don't know where you're going after this. But just now you're here, and so am I, and I don't want anything else in the world."

She was still there when Carys and Gareth came out to see why she was taking so long. She was dimly aware of them saying what a shame it was to wake her up – then they were helping her gently to her feet, and telling her that somebody called Jill had come to take her and Lily home.

Chapter Thirteen

Teasel stands in the box with her head down, but she does not kick or cry out. It's still a box, but it is wide and does not bump, and, above all, she has a friend. Hattie is here! This was unexpected, and the joy of seeing her old friend has given her courage. Hattie doesn't mind the box, and Hattie's only a donkey. So she stands still in the box, feeling the warmth of Hattie's rough coat beside her.

"The new tenants are moving into Mrs Tilney's house this week," said Mum. "I'm going to check it's all ready for them. Gwen, you'd better come with me – you're the one who knows your way around that house."

Two weeks had passed since Gwen had brought Teasel down from the hill. Michael and Jill had driven to Travon, scooped up Lily from the hospital and Gwen from the stables, and taken them home. As the midnight bells rang in the New Year, Gwen fell into the soft white bed with the image of Teasel behind her eyes. Waking in the night, she was not sure whether she was in the kindly warmth of the Baileys' house or back in the straw, curled up against Teasel.

In hospital, the X-ray had shown a fracture on Lily's foot, and she was now in plaster up to the knee. She spent the next morning painting it as a tree trunk, with a mouse running up it and ivy trailing from the top.

Teasel, they were told, could stay where she was "for the time being". She didn't know how long "the time being" might be, but Mrs Tilney was satisfied that Teasel was happy there, so that would have to do.

By the time Gwen came home she was coughing, her eyes were streaming, and she had flu for a week. Mum made remarks about "what could she expect after a night in the cold and damp", but it seemed to Gwen that she was gentler than usual. Even Charlotte looked in now and again and asked if she was all right. Jack constantly brought her glasses of orange squash and home-made get well cards, and Robin drew her a picture of a pony. As she recovered she knew that her family cared about her, and it felt good. They even seemed to admire her for looking after Lily. Suddenly Charlotte talked to her as an equal.

On the Saturday morning when Mum called her to come to Mrs Tilney's house, she'd been back at school for most of the week. It might be good to see Mrs Tilney's house again. She'd have to face Teasel's empty paddock sooner or later. And poor Hattie would be alone now, and would be glad of company. She'd better take some carrots. Then Charlotte said that she wanted to come, too, which was surprising, and as Dad was working it meant that there was nobody at home to look after the twins. So all of them arrived at Mrs Tilney's house that day.

"The front door's open," she said as Mum parked the car outside. "The new people must be in already."

"You'd better go and say hello to them, then," said Mum, and they followed her up the path. Even though they were behind her, she was aware of a glance passing between Mum and Charlotte, and a suppressed little squeak as if Charlotte was trying not to laugh.

Gwen knocked shyly at the open front door, and pushed it. There was somebody in the hall.

"Lily!" she cried – and beyond Lily was Mrs Tilney, leaning on a stick and looking so happy that Gwen could almost see the young Mrs Tilney from the photographs. And Michael was there, and Jill—

"What's happening?" she asked.

She looked from one smiling face to another. Michael held open the kitchen door and she walked through it as if she were dreaming. The utility room door was open, and she stepped out into the paddock.

There she was.

Teasel stood alone in the field, light biscuit gold, and in the cold weather her coat was thick and soft. Her pale flaxen mane swept softly to one side as if she tried to look beautiful in spite of the weather, and she stood very still with one hoof tilted. On the other side of the fence stood Hattie the donkey with her waterproof cover over her back.

Gwen could not speak. This must be a dream, and Teasel would disappear. She walked towards her softly, as if she were afraid of breaking something. Then Teasel turned and whinnied and Gwen wrapped her arms around her and pressed her face against the warm neck.

After what may have been a long time, she looked up. Mrs Tilney, Lily and Michael were behind her. Lily was leaning on one crutch and holding on to Michael's arm for support, and Jack slipped his hand into Gwen's. Behind them in the doorway stood Mum, Charlotte, Jill and Robin, huddling together like conspirators and beaming.

"Why is she here?" she asked. "You've got tenants coming here."

"They're only renting the house," said Mrs Tilney. She clipped a lead rein on to Teasel's head collar. "Not the paddock. The paddock is for Teasel again. She's come home."

"She went into the horsebox as good as gold this time," said Michael. "They got a nice big roomy one and gave her plenty of time to get used to it. And Hattie helped."

"Hattie?" repeated Gwen.

Lily giggled. "Isn't Hattie a little cutie! We got her

up to Travon, to where Teasel was, and Teasel was so happy to see her again, she'd go anywhere with her. She was fine in there when she saw Hattie go in first."

"And now Teasel's home," said Mrs Tilney firmly.

"But you'll be living with Michael and Jill!" she exclaimed. "You won't get to see her!"

"My dear, I'm in no fit state to look after her now," said Mrs Tilney. "Anyway, she's not my pony. I kept her too long." She placed the lead rope in Gwen's hands. "She's your pony. All yours. I'll be happy, knowing she's in your hands."

It was as if everybody else faded away and there was nobody there but herself and Teasel. *Little golden pony. MY little golden pony. Nobody will take you away again.* And then for sheer joy and thankfulness, she flung her arms round the nearest person, who was Michael, and Lily nearly fell over.

When she had thanked everyone and hugged everyone, and done it again, and everyone had hugged her, she whispered something to Mum about how could they afford it, and Mum whispered back that the Baileys and Mrs Tilney had given them something for feed and vet insurance, and she wasn't to ask any more about it. And then Jill said something about drinks, and everyone drifted into the house except Mrs Tilney and Gwen.

Gwen stood back, and looked again at Teasel. She walked all round her carefully, keeping away from her hind legs. Then she ran her hand over Teasel's firm, rounded flank, once on each side, and looked at Mrs Tilney.

"She's rounder than she was," said Gwen. "She's not fat, but she's bigger."

"Yes," said Mrs Tilney. "That's what I thought. Well, there you are, that's nature for you. She was living on the hill from June to December."

"She was," agreed Gwen. "But then, what—"

"Now, young lady, don't you dare start talking about expense and all that stuff," ordered Mrs Tilney. "That's all taken care of."

Gwen stroked Teasel's nose. "You clever girl!" she said. And she wondered what her family would say when she told them that, as well as Teasel, she would have the foal to care for as well.

"It'll be fine," she said. "You're home."